"You Have To Make Love To Me,"

Sylvie told Chase in a whisper outside the conference room door.

"Now?"

"Well," she hedged, "according to the kit, ovulation will occur sometime within the next twenty-four hours. But it could be happening now."

"But you said it wouldn't happen until tomorrow. Or even Saturday. Couldn't we do this Saturday? I'm in the middle of something very—"

"So my timing was off," she interrupted. "I've been a little anxious lately. That can throw a woman's cycle off."

"But—"

"No buts," she told him. "We have to make love."

"Now?" he asked again.

"*Now.*"

Dear Reader,

This month we're filled with fabulous heroes, delightful babies, tie-in stories and a touch of the magical!

The MAN OF THE MONTH, *Mr. Easy*, is from one of your favorites, Cait London, who once again spins a love story in her own special way.

Next, we have *babies*. First, in *The Perfect Father*, another installment in the FROM HERE TO MATERNITY series by Elizabeth Bevarly, and next in Karen Leabo's wonderful *Beach Baby*.

For those of you who have been looking for the next episode of Suzanne Simms's HAZARDS, INC. series, look no more! It's here with *The Maddening Model*.

Peggy Moreland brings us a hero with a mysterious past—and a heroine with a scandalous ancestress—in *Miss Lizzy's Legacy*. And don't miss the very special *Errant Angel* by award-winning author Justine Davis.

This month—as with every month—if you want it special, sexy and superb, you'll find it...in Silhouette Desire.

Happy reading!

Lucia Macro
Senior Editor

Please address questions and book requests to:
Silhouette Reader Service
U.S.: 3010 Walden Ave., P.O. Box 1325, Buffalo, NY 14269
Canadian: P.O. Box 609, Fort Erie, Ont. L2A 5X3

ELIZABETH BEVARLY
THE PERFECT FATHER

SILHOUETTE *Desire*®
Published by Silhouette Books
America's Publisher of Contemporary Romance

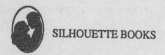 SILHOUETTE BOOKS

ISBN 0-373-05920-5

THE PERFECT FATHER

Copyright © 1995 by Elizabeth Bevarly

Books by Elizabeth Bevarly

Silhouette Desire

An Unsuitable Man for the Job #724
Jake's Christmas #753
A Lawless Man #856
A Dad Like Daniel #908
The Perfect Father #920

Silhouette Special Edition

Destinations South #557
Close Range #590
Donovan's Chance #639
Moriah's Mutiny #676
Up Close #737
Hired Hand #803
Return Engagement #844

*From Here to Maternity

ELIZABETH BEVARLY

is an honors graduate of the University of Louisville and achieved her dream of writing full-time before she even turned thirty! At heart, she is also an avid voyager who once helped navigate a friend's thirty-five-foot sailboat across the Bermuda Triangle. "I really love to travel," says this self-avowed beach bum. "To me, it's the best education a person can give to herself." Her dream is to one day have her own sailboat, a beautifully renovated older model forty-two-footer, and to enjoy the freedom and tranquillity seafaring can bring. Elizabeth likes to think she has a lot in common with the characters she creates, people who know love and life go hand in hand. And she's getting some firsthand experience with maternity as well—she and her husband recently welcomed their first-born baby, a son.

For Elias David Beard,
the new man in my life.
I love you, buckaroo.

Prologue

"Okay, Simon. Now do as Auntie Sylvie says, and everything will be just fine."

Sylvie Venner widened her eyes and nodded with encouragement, then guided a spoonful of strained carrots toward her eight-month-old nephew's mouth. She fingered a length of her blond blunt-cut hair away from her eyes and felt something gloppy sticking to the jaw-length tresses. When she pulled away her hand, she saw that her fingertips were covered with orange. Smiling indulgently, she placed the spoon back into Simon's bowl and reached for a napkin to wipe what she could of the carrots from her hair.

"You nailed Auntie Sylvie pretty well with that last handful, didn't you, buckaroo?"

Simon squealed with laughter and squirmed with delight in his high chair.

Olivia McGuane, Sylvie's sister and Simon's mother, glanced up from tossing a salad and smiled. "I told you he was an adventurous eater, and I told you not to feed him when you're dressed for work. But *nooooooo*. You had to be the one to do the honors."

Zoey Holland, a co-worker of Olivia's who completed the trio of very close friends enjoying their monthly Sunday-afternoon brunch, laughed. "Nice sweater," she said of Sylvie's thick, bright red, hand-crocheted cardigan. "How much did you pay for it?"

Sylvie sighed as she inspected the garment in question. In addition to her sweater, her bartender's uniform of white dress shirt, multicolored silk necktie and black, man-style trousers was also decorated by a number of other colors—beet purple, string-bean green, tapioca off-white and squash yellow. Each had been a course she'd been certain the baby would love, but Simon had sent them all back, deeming them—in his own unique way—unsuitable fare.

"I got this sweater on sale, all right?" she replied. "Besides, baby food is organic. The dry cleaner can get it out. Right, Livy?"

Olivia's expression was not reassuring. "Actually, I'm not sure what they make baby food out of. Whatever it is, it bears absolutely no resemblance to real food."

Zoey nodded her agreement. "I think there's some hush-hush, top secret lab somewhere in a place like Spongemop, South Dakota, that biochemically engineers baby food to be as offensively tasting and eternally staining as possible."

"I've read that, too," Olivia confirmed with a nod.

Sylvie eyed her friend and her sister warily. Both women worked as R.N.'s in a hospital maternity ward—Zoey in the nursery and Olivia in obstetrics. They probably knew what they were talking about. She threw Simon a suspicious look. He threw a suspicious look of his own right back at her. Then he smiled a two-tooth smile, revealing his dimples, and Sylvie forgave him his transgressions.

"Do you think he'll ever grow any hair?" she asked, noting the bald scalp with which the little guy had been born.

Olivia shook her head, her own long dark curls flying. "Who knows? By this time I'm so used to him bald, I'm not sure I'd recognize him with hair."

Zoey shoved a fat, auburn braid over her shoulder and snatched a deviled egg from a plate full of them on the table. "He's getting cuter every day, Liv. You should list him with a talent agent. If nothing else, he could be a 'before' shot on one of those late-night commercials for that men's hair-growing club.''

Sylvie chuckled. "Well, all I know is that it looks like Auntie Sylvie's going to have to try a new tactic if she's going to get the little buckaroo fed." She lifted the spoon into her hand once more, then vibrated her lips together to simulate the sound of an engine.

Simon smiled at her, looking intrigued.

Sylvie smiled back. Maybe she was on to something here. "Cooperation, buddy. That's today's word. Now, open your mouth and let Mr. Airplane fly right inside."

The baby did as requested until Sylvie's hand was within millimeters of completing the task. Then Simon shut his mouth tight, crossed his pudgy arms over his stomach and turned his head to the side. Sylvie couldn't help but laugh at his expression.

"Oh, boy, Simon. You're definitely Venner through and through. Neither your mama nor your auntie ever does anything she doesn't want to do."

"And when your aunt *does* want something," Olivia added, "watch out. Because nothing—and I mean *nothing*—is ever going to make her change her mind about going after it."

"Must be some genetic thing," Zoey said.

Simon cooed and gurgled his agreement.

Sylvie set the bowl of carrots on the kitchen table beside her. Simon had eaten almost as much as he'd thrown on her, she decided, which meant he'd eaten quite a bit. She pulled him out of his high chair, told the others she was going upstairs to clean up both herself and the baby, and departed with the little guy in tow.

Simon was such a wonderful baby, Sylvie thought as she fastened the Velcro closures on his diaper some time later. He stared up at her from his changing table, his ridiculously long lashes making his wide brown eyes appear even darker. He kicked his legs and circled her index finger with one hand. Then he blew a bubble and smiled at her again.

"He's pretty cute, huh?" Zoey asked as she entered the nursery and looked over Sylvie's shoulder.

"The cutest baby in the world," Sylvie agreed.

"And the smartest," Olivia added as she joined the other two.

For a long moment all three women stared down at Simon, and his gaze wandered intently over each face. When he refused to release Sylvie's finger, she lifted her other hand to his cheek, stroking the warm, delicate skin softly with the pad of her thumb.

"I need to tell you guys something," she said suddenly. She hadn't intended to break the news to her friends just yet, but for some reason the moment seemed right. "I'm going to have a baby."

She looked up to find Olivia and Zoey gazing back at her with identical expressions of undeniable surprise. Or shock, maybe, Sylvie amended. Shock was probably a more accurate assessment of their reactions.

"A baby?" Olivia asked.

"When?" Zoey demanded.

"Soon," Sylvie told them. "Christmas, I think. That would be a nice time to have a baby, don't you think?"

"But Christmas is more than eleven months off," Zoey pointed out. "I think your math might be just a little skewed here, Sylvie. Or else you're dumber than you look."

Sylvie made a face at her.

"Uh, not as smart as you look?" Zoey amended.

Still Sylvie stared.

"Well, you do realize it only takes about nine months to make a baby, don't you?"

"I know that," Sylvie assured her.

"But you're not... there's no one... I mean..." Olivia drew a deep breath and tried again. "Okay, little sister, if you're going to have a baby, then who's the father? Although you certainly go out often enough that you've got a passel of guys to choose from, I know for a fact that you've almost never found one interesting enough to... you know. Don't tell me there's someone special after all this time."

Sylvie smiled cryptically. "I haven't quite decided who the father is yet."

Her two companions turned to look at each other, then back at Sylvie. Olivia lifted a hand and cupped it gently over her sister's forehead.

"No fever that I can detect," she told Zoey. "So it must be some kind of psychological trauma."

"It's neither," Sylvie assured them, pushing her sister's hand away. "I *am* going to have a baby. In late December. And I don't know yet who the father is."

"I'll get Dr. Clifferman on the phone," Zoey said as she turned her attention to Olivia. "He's the best shrink in town. You get the straitjacket. Just don't make any sudden moves around her."

"Will you guys knock it off?" Sylvie said. "I'm not crazy. I'm not pregnant yet, either. But I will be soon."

The other women looked at her again, but this time their commentary was a bit more subdued.

"Why on earth would you want to get pregnant?" Olivia asked. "Trust me, I know what I'm talking about. Those nine months are no picnic in the best of circumstances—let alone when you're single and have no idea what to expect."

Sylvie shrugged. "But I want to have a baby."

"Don't you think it might help to find a father for this baby first?" Zoey suggested. "And fall in love with him first? And marry him first? That's the way things tradition-ally happen, even in this, the very late twentieth century."

"I'm not a traditional person," Sylvie said.

"Well, that's certainly true," her sister agreed.

"And I have no interest in attaching myself permanently to a guy. They bring nothing but trouble. You, Livy, above anyone, should know that."

"Hey, what I know is that I'm now married to the most wonderful man in the world and can't wait to make his children Simon's siblings," Olivia told her. She held up a hand to ward off her sister's objection as she added, "Oh, I won't deny I made more than a few mistakes before Dan-iel entered the picture, but... That's all the more reason to be reassured there's some perfect guy out there for you, too. Just give it time, Sylvie."

Sylvie shook her head. "Daniel's one in a gazillion. There aren't any others like him in the world. And there certainly isn't a man in the world who could make me change my mind about staying single. I *like* being single. But I'd also like to be a mother. Being around Simon has stirred up something inside of me I've never felt before. It's a wonderful feeling, Livy. I know—way down deep in my heart I'm absolutely certain—that I'm destined to be a mother. And I'll be a good mom, too. I just know I will.''

''We're not disputing that,'' Zoey said, her voice softer now. ''You'll be terrific with kids of your own. It's this father business we're worried about.''

Olivia nodded her agreement. ''You know how I feel about this, Sylvie. Mine and Daniel's situation after Simon was born could have filled a book. You have to be careful. Having a child isn't something you can go into without considering all the repercussions in advance.''

Sylvie lifted her chin defensively. ''You did.''

''Yeah, and look how much grief it caused me.''

''But everything turned out with a 'happily ever after,' didn't it?''

She knew Olivia couldn't dispute that. She and her husband were two of the happiest people Sylvie knew. But there was another, stronger reason she was in such a hurry to become a mother. And, she decided as she thought about it, she supposed Livy and Zoey deserved to know.

''There's something else,'' she finally said quietly. ''Something more that makes me eager to have a baby now, as soon as possible. I really don't have much choice.''

Olivia and Zoey eyed her warily. ''Why not?'' they asked as one.

Sylvie sighed. She still hadn't quite come to terms with it herself. ''I don't have much time left to make a baby,'' she said.

''Why not?'' the other two women repeated.

''I went to the gynecologist last week, and she verified something that she's suspected for a long time. Evidently I've been having some problems with my reproductive plumbing. Dr. Madison seems to think that I've only got about a year left that I can truly count on being fertile. After that, it's going to be increasingly difficult for me to get pregnant. If I'm going to have a baby, I have to do it now.

Otherwise, there's a chance I might never be able to conceive."

"Sylvie, we need to talk more about this," her sister said. "And you need to *think* more about this. Think long and hard before you make a final decision."

"I've already thought about it long and hard," Sylvie assured the other women. "And I've already made my final decision. My baby will arrive just in time for Christmas."

"And the father?" Zoey asked in a tone of voice that indicated she was no more enthusiastic about Sylvie's decision than Olivia was.

Sylvie smiled. "I have two whole months to decide who among the men I know will make the best father."

"Two months," Zoey repeated, her expression illustrating how crazy she thought the whole idea was.

"Two months," Sylvie echoed with a decisive nod. "That's all the time I'll need to find the perfect father for my child."

One

Cosmo's Bar and Grille had been a downtown Philadelphia fixture for decades, a five-star restaurant known for its continental fare, its soothing peach-and-gray art deco atmosphere and its continual showcase of good jazz music. But those weren't the only reasons Chase Buchanan liked to frequent the place. As he made himself comfortable at his usual spot at the bar, he caught the bartender's eye. Without even asking him what he was drinking, she reached for a bottle of expensive single-malt Scotch and splashed a generous portion over ice in a crystal tumbler.

"Hi, Mr. Buchanan," she said as she placed the glass before him with a cheerful smile.

"Hello, Sylvie," he replied.

"I was beginning to think you weren't going to show up tonight. I should have known you were just working late. Again."

"Sometimes that's what it takes to get the job done."

She shook her head slowly, chin-length blond tresses shimmering with the motion. "You work too hard," she told him bluntly. "People should work to live, not live to work. You ought to stop and count your blessings some-time."

"Thanks, but I'd rather stop and count my change."

Sylvie shook her head at him again and simply repeated, "You work too hard."

Chase could hardly contradict her, not that he wanted to. Ever since he'd left his position as a junior architect of Bulwar-Melton-Jones Associates to start his own firm, he couldn't recall a moment when he hadn't had some major project commanding virtually every scrap of his time. BMJ had been a company without foresight, a bunch of old men with absolutely no imagination. He'd joined them immediately after receiving his college degrees and left them less than five years later. In the fifteen years that had followed, he'd made an excellent name for himself in the field of architectural design. His own company was known for its savvy, its cutting-edge timing and its farsighted vision. He had enough going on at any given moment to demand his complete and utter attention.

Buchanan Designs, Inc. meant everything to Chase. He gave 110 percent to his company. And dammit, he didn't expect any less from anyone who worked for him.

"Yes, well, that's easy for you to say," he finally told Sylvie after an idle sip of his drink. "You don't have to run this place."

Her smile broadened. "You couldn't pay me enough to run this place," she countered. "You couldn't pay me enough to run *any* place. I don't want to be in charge of anything. I don't want that kind of responsibility. Too much stress. That'll send you to an early grave faster than anything else will, you mark my words." She slung a linen towel over her shoulder and reached into the garnish bin to pop an olive into her mouth. "Not only that," she added carelessly, "but it eats up way too much of your time. There's a lot more to life than working, you know. And I intend to enjoy every moment of it I can."

Although he wanted to disagree with her, Chase didn't dispute her words. He was quite certain that what Sylvie said rang absolutely true—for Sylvie. But he thrived on being in charge of his own company. For him, working *was* living. And he was perfectly happy with things that way.

"Living means something different for everyone," he told her. "For me, and for everyone who comes to work for me, business has to come first. It has to be the one thing in life that's important. Hell, it has to be life, period."

She surveyed him intently. "If you ask me, that's nuts."

"I don't recall asking you," he said with a smile.

Normally, no one—absolutely *no one*—spoke to Chase so frankly and dogmatically. They didn't dare. But the attitude was perfectly normal coming from Sylvie. He expected it, and he more than tolerated it—he welcomed it. On more than one occasion she had been his devil's advocate, and the byplay he enjoyed with her was something he shared with no one else.

What was odd was that Chase really didn't know Sylvie all that well—hell, he didn't even know her last name. But he'd been coming into Cosmo's after work three or four times a week ever since he'd moved his office into the building across the street. That had been two years ago, and at that time, Sylvie had just been starting her own stint at the restaurant.

Somewhere along the way he had altered his schedule to match hers, stopping by for dinner at the restaurant before heading home only on those evenings when he knew she would be working behind the bar. Why he'd done this he didn't know. But Chase liked Sylvie. He liked her a lot. She was funny and spirited and a welcome change of pace after a long day of stress and high pressure. She was cute in her man's white dress shirt that always appeared to be two sizes too big, and the neckties she wore with her uniform were always something interesting. She had a nice smile. And somehow she always made him feel better before he went home at night. Already he sensed the day's tension and irritation easing from every corner of his mind.

He'd even come close to asking her out a couple of times. But he never had. Because he just didn't date women for very long, and he hadn't wanted to put an end to the easy camaraderie he shared with Sylvie.

When he looked up from his drink she was eyeing him thoughtfully, and he wondered what was going on in that beautiful blond head of hers.

As if she sensed his inquisitiveness, she asked, "Are you telling me you'd rather work fifteen or sixteen hours a day than go home after the usual nine-to-five to a wife and family?"

Chase grimaced, running a big hand through coal black hair liberally threaded with silver. "God forbid. What a nightmare. Look, I'm forty years old and rabidly single. What does that tell you?"

She shrugged, still smiling. "Maybe that you're not such a great catch after all?"

He gaped at her before chuckling. "Oh, thanks a lot. I'll have you know there have been plenty of women who have tried to wrestle me to the ground and have their way with me—their way usually culminating in a leisurely stroll down the bridal path."

"But you want none of it, is that it?"

He shook his head vehemently. "Absolutely not."

"Not even the pitter-patter of little feet? You're not one of those guys who wants to make sure he leaves his mark on the world in the form of a little Mr. Buchanan, Junior?"

He shuddered for effect. "God, no. I can't stand children."

Her brows arched in surprise. "Are you serious?"

"Absolutely. I mean, think about it. When they're babies, all they do is lie there and look at you, commanding that you do everything for them. When they're children, they're constantly into things they shouldn't be into—you have to watch them every moment of the day. When they're adolescents...hell, forget about *that*. And when they're adults, they're completely ungrateful for everything you ever did for them, for every sacrifice you ever made."

He sipped his drink again before continuing, "Don't tell me you're surprised by the way I feel. You don't exactly seem like the kind of woman who wants to be dragged down by a passel of kids. You seem to enjoy being single."

"Oh, I love being single. But I also love kids." She bent beneath the bar and appeared to be searching for something, then rose again with a wallet in her hand. She flipped it open and thumbed through a bulging collection of photographs housed in the plastic sheets contained within. "This is my nephew, Simon," she said as she opened her wallet on the bar before Chase. "He's the most wonderful baby in the world. Look at that smile. You can't tell me you don't think he's adorable."

Chase offered the photo a perfunctory scan, pretended to be interested and replied dryly, "Adorable. Look, I'm starving. What's good tonight?"

Sylvie sighed and shook her head at him again. She seemed to be doing that a lot this evening, he thought. As if she were considering him for some major project only to find him lacking in some way. Or maybe not lacking, he amended when she continued to study him as she put her wallet away. That look in her eye was distinctly... interested.

He pushed the supposition away. Probably he *was* working too hard lately. No doubt he was thoroughly misreading the signals Sylvie was sending his way. She had never once offered him any indication that she wanted to get to know him better, and having heard her bemoan the shortcomings of some of the men in her life, he knew he was in no way her type.

And even if he was, even if she ever did come on to him, Chase knew he would never succumb. It was nothing personal, he reflected. If he were to get intimately involved with a woman right now, he supposed Sylvie was a likely enough candidate to fit the bill. But involvements led to entanglements, and entanglements led to relationships. And relationships, he thought, simply commanded too much time to keep them running properly. Time was a precious commodity. He had very little of it to spare. Therefore a relationship with a woman was the last thing he could afford.

Watching Sylvie as she strode to the end of the bar for a menu, he sighed wistfully. But maybe he had gone too long without the intimate aspects of a relationship, he conceded. When was the last time he'd made love to a woman, anyway? he asked himself now. And who was the last woman he'd made love to? He thought back, trying to recall the details.... His eyes widened when he remembered. No, surely it couldn't have been that long ago, he told himself. Could it? He shook his head in disbelief. Obviously he really *didn't* have time for a relationship.

If only he could find a nice woman with whom he could share a brief, one- or two-time interlude and call it quits. Unfortunately, most of the women who could provide such an encounter did it for a living, and that wasn't exactly the kind of woman Chase had in mind. He couldn't make love to a stranger, nor to someone who chose sex for her occupation. For his fantasy fling, he wanted a woman he cared for to at least some degree—and who cared for him in return—but who wouldn't demand all of his attention after it was over.

"Yeah, right," he muttered to himself. And what self-respecting woman would concede to an arrangement like that? No one of his acquaintance, that was for sure.

He looked up from his drink and saw Sylvie standing before him, holding a menu out for his inspection.

"Sounds wonderful to me," she said. "Want to give it a try?"

For one wild moment Chase thought she was offering herself up for just the kind of hit-and-run encounter he had just been imagining. Then he realized she must have been talking to him for several moments without his listening, and that he'd only heard the conclusion of her speech.

"What?" he asked. "I'm sorry, I was thinking about something else. Could you go over that again?"

She gazed back at him with much interest, and he just couldn't shake the feeling that she was evaluating him in some way. However, when she spoke, her voice held its usual careless timbre, and the choices she offered him were anything but erotic in nature.

"I was telling you that Cosmo is really pushing the free-range chicken tonight, and having had it for dinner myself, I can tell you it's delicious. But the shrimp *étouffée* also sounds wonderful to me. I know you love seafood. You want to give that a try instead?"

Chase gazed at her for a moment before replying, noting for the first time that Sylvie really did have the most beautiful blue eyes he'd ever seen. Not a pale, glassy blue, but a deep, midnight blue that bordered on violet. He didn't know why he hadn't noticed before.

"Uh, surprise me," he finally said, not altogether certain he was talking exclusively about his dinner selection. "I'm not really sure what I want."

"Okay."

As she turned to ring up his order, he observed with much interest the efficiency of her actions. He liked to watch Sylvie. She moved freely and easily, completely unconscious of her own gestures, utterly comfortable in her surroundings and with herself. That was something Chase had never quite been able to master in himself. There was still a lingering essence of self-consciousness within him, a quiet little voice that would never quite let him forget the meagerness of his beginnings or the fear that he might end up a nobody.

Yet he never tried to completely quell his fears. Because he knew they were what caused him to be so driven. Success and wealth had come to him earlier than he had anticipated, and now that he'd had a taste of how good life could be, he'd be damned if he'd ever do anything to jeopardize his position.

Even if that meant spending the rest of his life alone, he thought. In the long run, he knew he'd be a happier man because of it.

After ringing in Mr. Buchanan's order, Sylvie handed it off to one of the waiters headed back to the kitchen, almost hitting her co-worker in the face with it as he passed. She apologized sheepishly as she spun back around. Business at Cosmo's that evening had been slow, even for a Tuesday night, but her timing had been off completely since coming in to work several hours ago. As she frequently did at times like this, she couldn't help wondering yet again why she hadn't put her degree in humanities to better use than tending bar.

Maybe, she decided as she ran a blue grease pencil under the last of the drinks orders at the service bar, it was because no matter how hard she looked, there was never, *ever* a listing in the classified ads under the heading Humanities.

"Order up, Sylvie."

She spun around to find one of the waiters scooting a plate of oysters Rockefeller precariously close to the edge of the bar, and she snatched it up just as it was about to go over the side.

"Keith!" she called out to the swiftly departing server after she'd placed the appetizer in front of a well-dressed couple seated at the bar.

Keith turned. "What is it? I'm in the weeds big time."

She threw him what she knew was her most beguiling smile. "Got a minute?"

He smiled back as he returned to the bar. "Sure. But just one. And just because it's you who's asking."

She tried to feign a more intimate interest in him. "Mind a personal question?"

His smile broadened. "How personal?"

"You, uh, you graduated from Princeton, right?"

He nodded.

"And you're going to Villanova now? Law school?"

Another nod. "What's this leading up to, Sylvie?"

She extended her index finger onto the bar, coyly drawing a few idle circles in the remnants of a spilled beer. "What, um...what's your G.P.A?"

"Three point ninety-eight. Why?"

Sylvie looked at him, taking in his blond hair, blue eyes and slender build. Nice genes, she thought. And his coloring was identical to hers, so if she asked him to father her child, the baby would resemble her no matter what. "Oh, I was just thinking," she began again. "I need to ask you about some—"

Her words ceased when Keith cried out, bent over suddenly and cupped a hand over his left eye.

"What?" she asked, alarmed. "What's wrong?"

"Nothing," he muttered as he straightened. He manipulated his left eyelid gently over a red, watery eye. "I just got something in my contact. It's okay now."

Sylvie studied him more closely. "You wear contact lenses?"

"Yeah, I'm blind as a bat without them."

"Oh."

"Now, then," Keith continued, wiping away the last of the tears. His eye was still quite red and puffy. "What was this personal question you wanted to ask?"

"Your eyesight is really bad?" Sylvie asked.

"The worst. Everyone in my family has lousy eyesight. I don't think any of us made it out of childhood without getting a pair of glasses. Mine have lenses as thick as Coke bottles."

She nodded. "I see."

"And this personal question?" he asked again, clearly interested in getting as personal as possible with Sylvie.

"Uh," she hedged. "Never mind. I forgot what I was going to say."

His expression fell. "Oh. Well, if you remember..."

"I'll let you know."

When Keith was out of sight, Sylvie pulled a well-worn scrap of paper from inside her shirt pocket and unfolded it. Keith's name was midway down the list, beneath a half dozen or so others that had been crossed out. Leonard had been her first choice as the ideal candidate to father her child, but she'd learned he had recently become engaged. William, the second of her male acquaintances on the list, had just returned from a skiing trip with both arms and one leg in a cast. Jack, whose wavy brown hair she had loved, also had a brother in prison, and Sylvie simply didn't want to risk the felony gene turning up in any child of hers. Donnie, she'd discovered, had worn braces all through junior high and high school.

So far, none of the candidates Sylvie had considered with good genetic potential for fatherhood was working out at all. There always seemed to be *something* that just didn't quite set well. Edgar had been close, she recalled, but there was that big bump on the bridge of his nose that, despite his assurances to the contrary, she wasn't quite convinced he'd suffered in a fight. It might just be a congenital condition. And Michael...well, he had been just this side of perfect. But he'd confessed to having absolutely no musical inclination whatsoever. And Sylvie wasn't about to give birth to a no-talent child.

Yet there was still that question of the second set of chromosomes she would need to make a baby. There must be *someone,* she thought, looking down at the list again. Someone who would enjoy a little intimate rendezvous with her—maybe two, depending on how well it went the first time—and then get the heck out of her life. But who?

She glanced discreetly over her shoulder at Mr. Buchanan, the one person who frequented the bar whose nightly appearances she genuinely welcomed. Most of her regular customers were jerks, which was why she hadn't explored that group of men when considering potentially perfect fathers. But Mr. Buchanan, she thought now...

That little conversation the two of them had just enjoyed had pretty much reinforced everything she already knew about him. He had absolutely no desire to encumber himself with a family, because his work was his life. Therefore, should he be the one to father her baby, she wouldn't have to worry about him becoming all sappy and sentimental, wanting to play a role in the raising of that child. He was handsome, too, she noted, not for the first time, and he seemed the result of a better-than-average set of genes. She liked him. An intimate rendezvous with Mr. Buchanan wasn't outside the realm of possibility. Of course, it would help if she knew his first name.

She scanned the list in her hand once again. There were five names left, all of them men Sylvie didn't know particularly well. She wasn't sure she could make love with a man she scarcely knew, especially when she hadn't made love that often with men she knew extremely well. But time was running out. It was already the last week of February. She'd be ovulating again in two weeks. If she wanted a Christmas baby—and she did very much want a Christmas baby—she was going to have to find the perfect father for her child quickly.

"Order up, Sylvie. Shrimp *étouffée.* "

Her gaze traveled slowly from the plate of food a passing waiter placed on the bar to the man who had asked her to surprise him. And as she made her way slowly down the bar toward Mr. Buchanan, she began to study him in a way she never had before. When she set the plate before him, he looked up to murmur his thanks, and she found herself staring into clear green eyes full of intelligence.

She moved slightly away as he began to eat, but continued to observe him closely, noting with interest the expensively cut, jet black hair, the high cheekbones and perfectly sculpted jaw, the finely formed lips beneath a near-perfect nose that claimed not a chink. She had always thought Mr. Buchanan was very attractive. She considered him smart and ambitious. She also knew that although he was scarcely forty, he headed up one of Philadelphia's most prominent architectural firms.

When he turned to lift a hand in greeting to another regular at the bar, Sylvie studied his eyes in profile. No contacts, she noted. When he turned back to her, he caught her watching him and smiled, and she noticed that one of his front teeth was bent just the tiniest bit over the other. Not enough to mar his appearance in any way, but enough to let her know he'd never had orthodontic work done.

She pulled the pencil from behind her ear and added another name to the bottom of her list, drawing an arrow from the words *Mr. Buchanan* to the space immediately beneath Keith's name. Then she tucked the list back into her shirt pocket.

"Hey, Mr. Buchanan," she said thoughtfully as she reached for his empty glass to refill it for his usual second drink. "You know, there's something I've always wanted to ask you."

"What's that?" he asked.

"Do you play any musical instruments?"

Two

Chase was stumped. "Musical instruments?" he asked.

Sylvie nodded as she reached for a bottle of Laphroig from the mirrored shelves behind her. Had he become such a regular at Cosmo's that she didn't even bother to ask what he was drinking anymore, or if he even wanted a second? he wondered. Come to think of it, he couldn't in fact remember the last time she had asked him what had once been the lead-in to all their encounters. However, the question she was asking now was a new one.

"Yeah," she replied. "You seem like the musical type."

"Well, I played saxophone in my high school pep band," he confessed. "And I was part of a little jazz combo in college."

She smiled, and Chase felt ridiculously happy that he had said something to please her. "Really?" she asked. "Saxophone?" She seemed to consider something for a moment, then nodded in what he could only liken to approval. "Saxophone's cool."

"Well, I haven't played in years, of course—"

"But you were pretty good, right?"

He nodded, all modesty aside. "I was very good."

Sylvie's smile broadened as she placed his drink before him. "So tell me something else," she said.

"Yes?"

"How have you been feeling lately?"

He narrowed his eyes at her suspiciously. "I've been feeling fine lately," he told her. "Why? Do I look bad? Do you know something I don't?"

She shook her head. "Just wanted to make sure you're in good health."

"By my physician's latest account, my health is excellent, thanks."

"That's good to hear."

"Why so many questions?"

She studied him intently for a long time before answering, and suddenly Chase wasn't sure he wanted to hear her reply.

"Can I be honest with you?" she asked him.

"Of course."

She glanced around at their surroundings, at the two other bartenders and six or seven customers seated at the bar, at the flurry of waiters and waitresses who hustled around the service bar. His own gaze followed hers, and he wondered again what she was up to.

"I don't think we should talk about it here," she said. "But I'll be getting off at eleven if we don't get slammed any harder than this before then. Could I . . . could I maybe buy you a cup of coffee after my shift?"

Chase didn't know what to say. He'd never seen Sylvie in a social situation before. Come to think of it, he wasn't even sure he'd ever seen what she looked like from the waist down. Her invitation had come out of nowhere, completely unexpected. It unnerved him for some reason. He glanced down at his watch to find that it was just past ten. He'd have to wait an hour for her to finish up. Not that he had anything better lined up for the evening, he thought, but he probably ought to decline her invitation.

"Sure," he heard himself reply, wondering when he'd made the decision to accept her invitation instead.

She released a long breath and looked very relieved for some reason. "Great. I appreciate it. So, what do you think of the *étouffée*... ?"

A little over an hour later Sylvie sat opposite Mr. Buchanan at a tiny cocktail table in the corner of Cosmo's bar, clutching a cup of coffee as if it were a lifeline and feeling a little sick to her stomach. Was she crazy? she asked herself, studying the man opposite her as unobtrusively as possible from beneath her lashes. For the past hour she had completed her work behind the bar on automatic pilot, her thoughts instead whirling around one customer in particular.

What did she really know about Mr. Buchanan, anyway? she wondered. Not his first name, that was for sure. But he was handsome, intelligent and successful, had impeccable taste and knew how to play the saxophone. There didn't appear to be any one particular romantic interest in his life to prevent him from fathering her child. Although he'd come into Cosmo's a couple of times with a date, he'd never seemed to be with the same woman twice. As he himself had said, he was rabidly single.

He was older than her thirty years, she reminded herself further, by a full decade. And he was too much a workaholic to enjoy any kind of social or family life, something else that was a definite factor in Sylvie's favor. At his age, and with his occupation, he had no desire to be saddled by the responsibilities of fatherhood. If she had a child by him, there was no doubt in her mind that the baby would be hers alone.

But could she really ask him to do what she was thinking of asking him to do? Would she be able to go through with it herself if he agreed? Her stomach knotted painfully again. She tried to find reassurance by reminding herself how often she had thought her plan through, and how well she had everything under control. Unfortunately, when she looked into the cool green eyes of the big man seated across from her, she suddenly wondered if she really understood at all exactly what she was getting herself into.

"So, Sylvie," Chase began, uncomfortable in his realization that the two of them had been sitting at the table for more than five minutes without exchanging a single word. "What's on your mind?"

She was staring down into her coffee cup as if it held the answers to the secrets of the universe, her long blond bangs falling in a silky sheath over her forehead. A stray tress she had tucked behind one ear fell forward, too, and Chase suddenly wanted nothing more than to reach across the tiny table and push it back into place. He'd never really noticed how soft her hair appeared to be. But in the dim glow of the candle flickering on the table between them, everything about Sylvie suddenly seemed soft.

"I, uh," she began quietly. She inhaled deeply, and Chase waited to hear the rest. "I sort of have something I'd like to ask you."

"Another question?" he said, smiling when she continued to avoid looking at him. "You've had quite a few of those tonight."

She nodded. "I, uh . . ." She paused, inhaled deeply, released her breath slowly and tried again. "I, uh, I have an older sister," she began, finally glancing up, her gaze settling on his.

Good God, her eyes were blue, he thought again before the significance of her words struck him. Then he began to understand where all this was going. Oh, no. He'd heard that "I-have-a-sister/niece/cousin/dog groomer/hairdresser/whatever" speech before. Too many times. If Sylvie thought she was going to fix him up with her sister, she had another think coming. He'd had his fill of blind dates. Not only did they always backfire, he didn't have the time.

"A sister," he repeated blandly.

She nodded again. "She had a baby last year—that would be my nephew whose picture I showed you earlier this evening, and—"

"A baby?" Chase asked incredulously. Sylvie wanted to saddle him with a wife *and* a kid? What was she trying to do, wreck his life completely? What had he ever done to her? Hadn't he just told her a short time ago that a family was the last thing he needed messing up his happiness?

He held up a hand to halt any other big plans she might be hatching. "Hold it right there, kid," he instructed her, ignoring her frown at his use of the word *kid*. She probably wasn't that much younger than him, but Chase was suddenly feeling like an antique beside her. "I'm not interested in being fixed up with your sister. Or her baby."

Sylvie looked confused for a moment, but quickly recovered. She began to giggle, then the giggle became a chuckle, and the chuckle became full-fledged laughter. Chase couldn't help but smile, too. Clearly he had misunderstood what she was going to say. She had no intention of getting him involved with her sister. He felt much better knowing that.

"Livy's already happily married—I'm not trying to fix you up with her and her baby," she said, confirming his suspicions and allowing him to breathe much more easily and laugh a little himself. "I'm trying to fix you up with me and my baby."

Chase stopped laughing immediately. "What?"

Sylvie suddenly stopped laughing, too. She hadn't meant to blurt it out like that. Somehow the words had just jumped from her mouth. But now that they'd been spoken, she had nowhere to go but forward.

"I didn't know you had a baby," Mr. Buchanan said.

"I don't," she told him. "But ever since Livy had Simon, I've been thinking that I'd like to have a baby, too."

"Just like that?"

She shook her head. "Simon's nine months old now. I've been giving this a lot of thought ever since he was born. And according to my doctor, despite the fact that I'm only thirty, I don't have a lot of time left to have a baby. If I'm going to become a mother—and I do want very much to become a mother—I don't have time to sit around waiting for some potential husband who might not ever show up."

"So why are you telling me this?"

Sylvie looked up to find her companion staring at her with frank curiosity. He hadn't figured it out yet, she realized. She supposed what she was planning was rather unusual— asking a man to make love to her specifically so that she could become pregnant, and then get out of her life for good. There were probably a number of men who would say yes in an instant. The irony was, men like that were generally jerks. She wouldn't want a jerk for her baby's father, would she? Of course not. In an ideal world, she wouldn't have to worry about all this. But this wasn't an ideal world, was it?

"Because," she said, feeling the words getting stuck in her throat, "because you're nice looking, intelligent and talented, and..." She stared down at her hands, spread open on the table, then licked her lips nervously before concluding, "And I'd like my baby's father to pass all those qualities along to him or her."

His expression never changed, and she wasn't sure whether or not she'd made herself clear.

"Meaning?" he asked.

His eyes were speculative, and the corner of his mouth twitched only the slightest bit. Oh, he knew what she meant, Sylvie thought. He just wanted her to spell it out for him.

"Meaning," she tried to explain again, "that I'd like for you to be the father of my baby. I mean... if you'd consider it."

For a long time Chase said nothing, only continued to stare at Sylvie as if she were speaking a foreign language. Finally he began again, "Are you actually saying you want me to donate my..." He glanced quickly around, cleared his throat and tried once more, his voice noticeably lower when he continued. "You want me to donate my sperm so you can be artificially inseminated with it?"

"Oh, heavens, no," she assured him.

The fire that had flared to life in his midsection subsided some. Obviously he was misunderstanding whatever it was Sylvie was trying to say. Clearly she meant something else entirely. He only wished he could figure out what it was.

"I want you to make love to me," she said.

"You *what?*"

"In two weeks. That's when I'll be ovulating again."

The words didn't register immediately with Chase. He knew what he thought he'd heard her say, of course, but he couldn't quite believe she was saying what he thought he was saying. This time he was the one to stare down into his coffee without speaking. But his silence only seemed to inspire Sylvie, because she continued to prattle on nervously.

"Um, look, I know what you're probably thinking about me right now. I know you must be . . . you know, wondering what kind of woman would ask a virtual stranger to make love to her just to get her pregnant, but—"

"Oh, we're not really strangers," Chase interrupted her, looking up. He fixed his gaze with hers. "Are we, Sylvie?"

She lifted one shoulder in an odd kind of shrug, but said nothing. He had never noticed how small she was, he thought. How delicate looking. She'd always seemed so strong to him, so straightforward, so unwilling to back down. He wondered how long she'd been considering him for the task at hand. And he wondered why what she was suggesting, something that should be no more than an indecent proposal, was in fact so utterly appealing.

"After all the conversations we've had over the last two years," he continued, "how can you think of us as strangers? You talked me through that hostile takeover bid last summer, remember? I would have gone nuts if I hadn't had you to confide in. And I think your advice helped me ward the bastards off better than any other I received."

She smiled nervously. "Really?"

He nodded. "You were there for me when my dad died, too."

"And you helped get me through the loss of my mom," she added. "But you know what's weird? I don't even know your first name."

"And I don't know your last."

"Venner," she said immediately. "Sylvie Venner."

"Chase," he replied, extending his hand toward her. "Chase Buchanan."

Sylvie placed her hand gingerly in his and smiled. She wasn't sure, but she thought the two of them might just be making a deal.

It was after 2:00 a.m. when the closing bartender finally routed them from Cosmo's. Chase walked Sylvie to her car, both of them moving slowly in spite of the below-freezing temperature, as if they had nowhere in particular to go.

Downtown Philly was deserted this time of night, its chrome-and-glass high rises dark and vacant. She inhaled deeply, the scent of winter mingling with a hint of lingering bus fumes. The city seemed quieter than she knew it really was.

They had settled nothing for certain, she thought as she strode alongside him. Although she had spent much of the evening arguing her case eloquently and with forthright honesty, Chase hadn't agreed to her request. But he hadn't turned her down, either, she reminded herself. And he had seemed to enjoy their time together as much as she had.

When they reached her car she unlocked it, then tossed her purse into the passenger seat. She was about to pitch the book she'd been reading in her spare time in behind it, but he stayed her hand by circling her wrist with warm fingers.

"*The Portable Emerson?*" he asked when he saw the title, seeming not at all surprised by her choice of reading material.

Sylvie nodded. "I think *Nature* is one of the most wonderful series of essays ever written. I like to go back and reread it every now and then."

"I know what you mean," he said. "I love it, too."

She smiled. "I didn't know you were familiar with Emerson."

"He was part of my required reading in college. I was surprised by how much I liked him."

He released her hand, but not before skimming his fingertips lightly over the ridges of her bare knuckles. Sylvie shivered, uncertain whether it was because of his touch or the cold breeze rushing by.

"How come you never put your humanities degree to use?" he asked out of the blue.

She tossed the book in beside her purse, settled her arms on the open car door and rested her head on her overlapped hands. "I don't know. I always meant to go for my master's and then my Ph.D., thinking I would teach at a college level, but I just never got around to it. By the time I got my B.A., I was so sick of school I never wanted to go back. Now I'd love to go back, but I just don't have the time. Or the funds," she added with a philosophical shrug. "Maybe someday."

He nodded, but his mind seemed to be on something else.

"You know, you never really gave me a definite yes or no," she pointed out.

"No, I didn't."

Her heart fell. He wasn't going to do it, she thought, surprised at the depth of her disappointment. There were others on her list, she reminded herself. She still had a good chance of finding someone. But suddenly no one else seemed suitable. Chase Buchanan was it, she decided. The perfect candidate to father her child. If he said no, she didn't know what she would do.

"There's one thing I don't understand about this," he said further.

"What's that?"

"Why does the father of your child have to be someone you know? If you're so determined to have a baby, then why don't you just go the artificial insemination route? It's worked out fine for other women."

She nodded. "I know. And I did think about that as an alternative. I've heard you can virtually fill out an order form of what you expect from a donor and everything, but..."

"But what?"

She shrugged and looked away. His intense scrutiny was making her feel a little anxious. "That's not for me. I mean, I consider myself to be a thoroughly modern woman with thoroughly modern beliefs, and I certainly wouldn't fault any woman who chose that option. But... It's not for me," she repeated simply.

"Why not?"

She paused before elaborating, trying to think of the best way to make him understand. "It's just that... I guess I'm old-fashioned in a way, too. I don't have it in me to become impregnated while I'm lying on a metal table with my feet in stirrups and no one to share the experience but a team of experts in white coats, you know?"

He grimaced at her graphic description but said nothing.

"A baby should be conceived in a moment of affection," she went on softly. "Even if that moment only lasts...well, a moment. There should be some kind of positive emotion shared by the two parents, even if it's only temporary. At least, that's how *I* feel about it."

"Most people would say that the emotion involved should be a deep and abiding love that would last forever and unite the family as one," Chase said.

"I know that," Sylvie agreed, glancing away once more. "But I'm not convinced such an emotion exists."

When Chase said nothing, she looked at him again and could see that he was mulling over her statement. "Not that I disagree with you, but how come you feel that way?" he finally asked.

She shook her head resolutely. "I know there are those people who believe in love forever after," she continued. "Heck, my sister is one of the leading proponents. In fact, Livy being such a profound believer in the powers of love is probably why I'm so anxious to avoid it."

"Why's that?"

Sylvie hesitated before replying. Although it was true that Livy had finally found happiness with Daniel McGuane, it was also true that there was no other man in the universe like Daniel. Sylvie was certain anyway that *she'd* never find someone so utterly compatible with her own needs.

"Before Livy's husband came into her life, I watched her become involved with one guy after another—one loser after another—and she always ended up with a broken heart. I decided a long time ago that I would never let some bogus guy treat me the way men used to treat her. Uh-uh, no way, no how."

"But you yourself said she's happily married now," Chase observed. "Why don't you think the same thing will happen to you?"

"There's a big difference between me and Livy," Sylvie told him. "She's always wanted to be married. She's always wanted to have a man in her life. Me, I'm more independent. I don't want to be attached to anyone forever after. I don't want to find myself under any man's thumb."

"But having a baby would attach you to someone forever after. You'll be responsible for that child the moment it's conceived."

"That's different," Sylvie said with a smile. "Babies and children need you. They love you unconditionally, no matter what kind of minor character flaws you might have. They don't try to change you, they don't put restrictions on your emotions and they don't play mind games with you. That's not true of the men I've known."

Chase nodded thoughtfully, thinking her description of men fit perfectly what he'd always considered true of women. Interesting that they should share such identical philosophies about the opposite sex.

"Give me some time, Sylvie, okay?" he asked. "What you're suggesting is a little unorthodox, to say the least."

"I need to know within two weeks," she reminded him.

"Why the rush?"

"I want a baby for Christmas," she said, grinning.

She could see that there was still something troubling Chase, still something he didn't quite understand about her grand plan. "What is it?" she asked him.

"There's one thing we haven't discussed," he said, confirming her suspicion.

"And that is?"

He lifted a hand to brush her bangs back from her forehead, a surprisingly intimate gesture that she hadn't expected at all. His fingers were warm against her skin, his eyes revealing how unexpectedly the action had come to him, too.

His voice was soft when he said, "Where precisely will I fit in to the picture after my initial assignment is completed?"

"What do you mean?" she asked, her own voice sounding thinner than usual.

"After... after I make love to you, Sylvie..." He swallowed hard before he continued. "After you become pregnant, then what happens between me and you?"

"I guess we just go back to the way things were before."

"And do you honestly think we'll be able to do that?"

She sighed and stood straight, meeting his gaze as levelly as she could. "I don't know. I...I guess so. I mean, we probably can. You don't seem to want a woman in your life any more than I want a man in mine."

"That's true...."

"Which is all the more reason why this would be such a perfect arrangement. We've known each other for two years now and never put obligations on each other. There's no reason to think that has to change just because we happened to...to...make love...one time. Lots of people have brief sexual encounters and still remain friends." At least, Sylvie thought they did. It happened on television and in the movies all the time. Didn't it?

"That's true, too, but..."

Before Sylvie realized what was happening, Chase leaned forward and pressed his mouth to hers, his lips cool and confident at the initial contact. At first Sylvie was too startled to react, but when he tangled his fingers in the hair at her nape and pulled her more fully into the kiss, she couldn't help but respond. He was a good kisser, she decided immediately as she threaded her fingers through his hair, still not feeling as if they were close enough. Quite thorough at what he set out to do...

He pulled her away from the car door and more completely into his arms, plying her lips with his almost as if he were trying to devour her. He circled his other arm around her waist and splayed his hand open over the small of her back, urging her forward until she could almost feel the heat of him seeping through her clothes. She wasn't sure how long they stayed locked in their embrace, but one thing was certain—Sylvie never wanted it to end.

But it did end, as abruptly as it had begun. Chase pulled away and gazed at her, clearly confused, his ragged breathing mingling with hers to become a thin silver fog between them.

"I need a few days to think about it," he told her as he reluctantly released her. He set her away from him and pressed the back of his hand to his mouth before adding, "And I think you need a few days to think about it, too."

And with that he turned and walked away, without another word, and without a backward glance.

Sylvie watched him go, trying to understand the tumultuous emotions rocking her. Until a few moments ago she had been in complete control of the situation. She had planned every aspect down to the last detail and knew exactly how everything would turn out. Then Chase had kissed her, and her plans had dissolved, like the steam rising into the air with every uneven breath she took.

She had been so sure of herself before, she thought. But now she had no idea what she was supposed to do.

Three

———

Nearly one week after Sylvie Venner had asked him to act as her stud, Chase sat in his office actually mulling over the possibilities. He'd been able to think about little else in the past six days, after all. In fact, so focused had his thoughts been on the blond bartender that he'd scarcely given a single serious consideration to his business obligations, something that was in no way like him. He had deliberately avoided Cosmo's since that fateful conversation, uncertain how he would react the next time he saw Sylvie. And, to be honest, as surprised as he was to realize it, he sincerely didn't know what his answer to her should be when he did encounter her again.

A substantial segment of his psyche recoiled at the thought of being little more to a woman than the means to an end. The knowledge that there was only one part of him that Sylvie wanted, and only temporarily—and quite an intimate part at that—was startling, to say the least. There were moral and ethical considerations to ponder, as well. What was the world coming to, after all, when a woman sat across from a man she didn't know especially well and asked him to make love to her for the sole purpose of producing a child in whose life he would thereafter play no part? There was no question that he should decline her request, no question at all.

However . . .

Another part of Chase was more than a little intrigued by the idea. Hadn't he been sitting at the bar at Cosmo's that very night less than a week ago, wishing there was some way he could share a brief sexual encounter with a woman about whom he cared somewhat, then call the relationship quits with no harm done, no feelings hurt? And didn't what Sylvie had requested of him provide just the perfect opportunity for exactly that?

And deep down inside, he had to admit that there was something . . . oh, *arousing* . . . about the prospect of producing a child with Sylvie. A son, he thought, never questioning for a moment his conviction that the child he helped produce would be of the masculine persuasion. A strapping young boy rushing headlong into the world, whom he had been partly responsible for creating, but was in no way responsible for raising. Despite his belief that children were more trouble than they were worth, the possibility of creating one was understandably alluring for any man.

Of course, the child he and Sylvie produced would be a child with whom he would have no other contact, he mused further. He wasn't altogether certain he liked that idea. Then again, there were thousands of men out there who anonymously fathered children through donations to sperm banks without a second thought about it. On the other hand, Chase Buchanan wasn't one of them.

He rose from his chair, paced to the windows on the other side of the room and stared down at the busy street below. Why had Sylvie chosen him? he wondered for perhaps the hundredth time since hearing her suggestion. And why couldn't he just tell her he wanted no part of her plan, the way he knew he should, and be done with it once and for all?

Because deep down inside he couldn't quite rid himself of a sudden, shuddering desire to make love to Sylvie Venner. And not just because she wanted a child, he realized. And, he admitted further reluctantly, maybe not just because he felt a little lonely sometimes, either.

His mind still addled by all the implications of the situation before him, Chase straightened his tie, reached for his jacket and coat and, for the first time in his entire life, left work early.

Sylvie was baby-sitting her nephew, as she did every Monday in her downtown Philadelphia apartment, and had just finished feeding and cleaning up Simon after his nap when she heard the quick series of raps at her front door. She lifted the baby into her arms, adjusting his bright red playsuit and tugging at the yellow socks that refused to stay on completely, then went to greet her unexpected visitor. It was still a couple of hours too early for Daniel to be picking up Simon, but every now and then her brother-in-law left a construction site before the end of the day to retrieve his son on his way home.

To say she was surprised to view Chase Buchanan's face through the peephole would have been an understatement. She hadn't even told him where she lived. She wished he had given her some kind of warning, hated the fact that she was dressed in her most ragged jeans and a faded Princeton sweatshirt, now spattered with Simon's lunch, and wore neither makeup nor shoes. Dammit, she thought, why did men have to be so freaking difficult?

Just as she was tugging the front door open, Simon buried both fists in her hair and yanked hard in an effort to attempt what had become his latest quest—trying to pull himself up over her face toward the top of her head, presumably to sit atop her. Why a baby would want to sit on the top of her head, Sylvie had no idea. But as a result of his maneuvering, she was unable to greet Chase cordially, because her face was full of baby belly.

"Sylvie?" she heard his deep, resonant voice say.

Very gingerly she pushed Simon to the side and peeked around him. Sure enough, it was Chase Buchanan standing at her front door, dressed in all his power-suited glory and looking like a man who ruled the world. Immediately feeling self-conscious in her baby-sitting attire, not to mention the added accessory of said baby still fastened to her head, she stammered out something in greeting and tried to pull Simon away from her face.

"Uh, come on in," she said, stepping backward as she struggled to free the baby and lower him to her shoulder. "Long time, no see."

She had begun to wonder if she had scared Chase off forever after their little tête-à-tête last week. Although she'd searched for him every night, he hadn't returned to Cosmo's, and she'd been surprised to discover how much she missed seeing him on a regular basis at the restaurant.

With one final yank she managed to pry the baby from her head and lower him into her arms, pushing at her disarrayed hair with her free hand and hoping she didn't look *too* ridiculous. Then, unable to halt the question that formed so quickly in her brain, she added a little breathlessly, "What are you doing here?"

Chase strode past her and into the apartment, his eyes never leaving the baby who clung to her shoulders. Simon stared back, tucking his head warily into the curve of Sylvie's neck and chin, studying the stranger with a combination of curiosity and suspicion.

"I went to Cosmo's to see you, but then I remembered you have Mondays off," Chase said.

His gaze finally lifted to lock with hers, and Sylvie was once again struck by how clear and beautiful his green eyes were. She couldn't help but wonder why she'd never noticed them before.

"Mondays and Wednesdays," she said softly, unsure why she was bothering to remind him. "I sit for Simon on those days. It gives him a day off from day care. Plus, I just love doing it. Um, how did you find out where I live?"

"Well, no one at the restaurant was willing to part with the information, that's for sure," he said stiffly, as if insulted that he was in no way trusted by the wait staff of an establishment into which he'd pumped a considerable portion of his income over the past two years. "So I looked in the phone book. There was only one S. Venner listed. I took a chance that it was you."

She nodded. "Very resourceful."

"Not really."

Chase took a step toward her and studied the baby again. "So this is your nephew, the one who's made you completely rethink the issue of motherhood."

Sylvie smiled. "Chase, meet Simon McGuane. Simon, this is Chase Buchanan. He's a friend of mine, so you can trust him."

Chase glanced up when she introduced him as her friend, and she wished she could tell what he was thinking. He had a funny expression on his face, one she was in no way able to decipher. So she smiled experimentally, only to become more confused at the brief twitching of his own mouth in return.

The baby in her arms broke the tension of the moment by reaching a chubby hand out toward Chase. "Bob?" he said quietly.

Chase frowned, glaring at Sylvie. "Bob?" he repeated. "Who the he—" He stopped abruptly in deference to the little ears. "Who's Bob?" he asked.

She laughed. "No one. 'Bob' is Simon's favorite thing to say. He can make other sounds—dada, mama, gigga, babba, abba... all that important baby conversation—but 'bob' is by far his favorite."

"Bob," Simon said again as if to reinforce her explanation. He wiggled restlessly, and Sylvie bent to sit him on the floor. Immediately he maneuvered himself onto all fours. "Bob-bob-bob-bob-bob," he sang out merrily as with quick, deft movements he crawled toward a quilt spread open on the other side of the living room that housed a variety of brightly colored plastic toys.

Chase watched the baby go, marveling at what a splash of colorful incongruence Simon's play area was in the otherwise sleek, neutral, sophisticated furnishings of Sylvie's high-rise apartment. Along with that, he took in the padded corner protectors on the coffee and end tables, and the complete absence of knickknacks from the bottom three shelves of her bookcases—items that had been mingled haphazardly elsewhere in the room on higher ground. More toys were scattered about the floor—on the sofa, under tables, poking out from beneath chairs—and a cardboard book with a puppy on the front, whose corners looked suspiciously gummed, lay neglected near his feet.

He was surprised that a woman who clearly preferred clean lines and minimal furnishings would allow such a clutter in her home. Then he turned to see Sylvie staring after the baby with such obvious love and devotion etched on her face that he ceased to wonder at all.

When Simon plopped himself down on the quilt and contented himself with a fistful of something that resembled a green plastic doughnut, Sylvie turned to Chase again, and he was chagrined that she caught him staring at her. A rush of pink stained her cheeks as she hastily looked away and jabbed a thumb over her shoulder toward the kitchen.

"Would you like a cup of coffee?" she asked, sounding nervous for some reason. "It wouldn't take but a minute. I have some of those International kinds if you like. You know, the kind you use to celebrate the moments of your life? Or is that Kodak film that does that?" she prattled on nervously. "Or AT&T? Gosh, all those advertisements run together sometimes, don't they? Maybe it's Hallmark or Coca-Co—"

"Sylvie," Chase interrupted her quietly.

She shoved a hand anxiously through her bangs as she looked at some point over his shoulder. "What?"

All at once Chase was at a complete loss. He had no idea what he'd intended to tell her, why he'd come over to her apartment or why he suddenly never wanted to leave. "I...is it all right if I stay for a little while? I think we need to talk some more about this...this...this proposal you offered me."

He could see that she was surprised to discover he was still considering it. Surprised and clearly delighted.

"Of course you can stay for a while. Stay for dinner if you'd like. I think I have a couple of steaks in the freezer that I could thaw in the microwave. And there's stuff for a salad. A couple of potatoes. I'm not a gourmet chef by any stretch of the imagination—I usually eat at Cosmo's before I start work—but I can whip up the basics when hard-pressed."

Chase knew he should decline, knew he should discourage any further contact with Sylvie Venner that was anything other than casual, especially since he'd come to tell her that he couldn't possibly be the man who would father her child. Instead, he found himself shrugging out of his coat and suit jacket, tossing them with much familiarity over a nearby chair and loosening his tie to unbutton his collar.

"Only if you let me help you with dinner," he also heard himself say agreeably. "I, on the other hand, am a more than fair cook."

"You got it," she told him with a smile.

"And coffee sounds good for a start. But just the regular stuff is fine."

As Sylvie busied herself in the kitchen, Chase made himself comfortable on the end of the sofa nearest Simon. The baby seemed oblivious to his presence, however, so intent was he on the workings of a round toy filled with clear liquid and a variety of multicolored floating animals. Chase couldn't remember the last time he'd been this close to a baby. Perhaps he never had. And he was frankly surprised to find himself so captivated by the little guy after such a short exposure to him.

"How old is Simon?" he called out to Sylvie.

"Almost ten months," she replied. "He'll be one in May. He's pretty cute, huh?"

Chase nodded absently. "Yes," he said softly. "Yes, he is."

As if he knew he was the subject of the conversation, Simon glanced up and made a noise with his lips that sounded like a minuscule boat, then squealed with laughter at his own success. He waved his toy heartily at Chase before sticking it into his mouth, then sat perfectly still as he considered the bigger man. There was something about the baby's expression, something about his clear, guileless, uninhibited gaze, that thoroughly unsettled Chase. But not in a way that made him anxious or uncomfortable, he realized. Instead, the baby's obvious acceptance of him made Chase feel inexplicably good. Just . . . good. Good in a way he'd never felt before. It was an odd sensation.

"Coffee should be ready soon," Sylvie said as she seated herself in a chair opposite Chase on the other side of Simon. With a resolute sigh she leaned forward and rested her elbows on her knees, propping her chin in one hand as she dangled the other between her legs. "Now," she continued, "back to what we discussed last week."

Her plunge right to the point made Chase squirm involuntarily in his seat, and he tried to settle himself back against the overstuffed cushions in feigned comfort. Had he actually been the one to suggest they discuss this matter? he wondered. But before he could say a word, Sylvie began to talk again.

"I know you probably still have a lot of questions," she said, "not the least of which is making certain you'll be protected in this matter."

"Protected?" he asked, confused. He sat forward again, his attention wandering once more to the baby playing on the floor.

"From legal liabilities," she said in a matter-of-fact way that didn't sit well with Chase. "I realize you don't know me that well, and you're probably scared I'm going to hunt you down in fifteen or twenty years and demand thousands of dollars from you to pay for college or a wedding or some such thing."

She scooted forward to the edge of her chair, as if trying to emphasize what she had to say next. "I just want to reassure you right now that I have no intention of ever tapping into your financial resources for this baby. I make great money at Cosmo's, and he has a wonderful insurance plan. My finances are in order, and I'm fully prepared and capable of raising a child on my own. Once I'm pregnant, that will be the end of any obligation you have to me or the baby. I'll never bother you again for any reason. And I'm perfectly willing to sign any kind of document that would free you from all responsibility, financial or otherwise."

Chase stared at her in amazement. He honestly hadn't given that aspect of their arrangement a single thought. It made sense, of course. Naturally a man would want to be sure he didn't get taken for a ride in a case like this, especially when it was the woman who wanted the child and not him. But as surprised as he was to realize it, something in him balked at the idea of relinquishing all responsibility for the baby he would help Sylvie create. It didn't seem proper somehow, in spite of the way things had come about. It just didn't seem right.

"But—" he began to object.

"And of course, I'll expect the same courtesy of you," Sylvie went on. "I'd like you to grant me the same assurance that you won't come looking for me ten or fifteen years from now because you're going through some midlife crisis and feeling your mortality and wanting to share in my child's life. I think that's only fair, don't you?"

"I suppose. But—"

"We really do have to think of the child's best interests in this case, don't we? It wouldn't be fair to her, or him, to disrupt her, or his, routine so late in life, would it?"

"No, I guess not. But . . ."

She inhaled deeply and met his gaze levelly, looking to Chase as if she were terribly uncertain and more than a little scared. Somehow, he got the feeling that she wasn't nearly as confident of the things she was telling him as she was letting on.

"Then . . . then you'll do it?" she asked quietly.

The tone of her voice when she uttered the question gave Chase the feeling that Sylvie still wasn't sure *she* wanted to go through with it. He knew what he should do. He knew what he should tell her. He knew it would be a colossal mistake, not to mention a violation of ethical human behavior, to do what she was asking him to do.

But instead of looking at Sylvie when he responded, Chase's gaze fell to the baby boy sitting on the floor, who was busily stuffing a red cloth building block into his mouth. When he saw that Chase was looking at him, Simon pulled the toy away and curled his lips into a huge smile. For the first time, Chase noted the four tiny teeth jutting from the baby's gums, two on the top and two on the bottom. Then Simon laughed, a rough, cooing, joyous sound, his pale brown eyes and tiny nose crinkling with the action. That expression transformed the baby's face, turning it into one of the most delightful sights Chase had ever seen, and he couldn't help himself when he smiled in return.

Then, much to his amazement, he heard himself tell Sylvie, "All right. I'll do it."

"Okay, I think that takes care of most of the particulars," Sylvie said some time later as Chase topped off their glasses with the last of the cabernet.

They sat at her kitchen table, all remnants of dinner either stowed in the fridge or ready for a spin in the dishwasher. Daniel McGuane had come for his son and gone hours ago, and now the couple was alone. A legal pad and two pencils lay between them on the table, several of the yellow pages filled with two vastly different types of penmanship where either Sylvie or Chase had remembered something that should go into the legal document they intended to have drawn up. A legal document they would both sign, and which would formally seal the deal they had made only hours before.

Sylvie felt strange as she skimmed over the finer points of the contract. She had wanted for so long to find the perfect father for her child, had spent so many weeks searching for just the right candidate. Now that she had him, she was suddenly uncertain what to do next.

"Can you think of anything else?" she asked, indicating the legal pad as she reached for her glass.

Chase shook his head. "No, I think this about covers everything. I'll have my attorney draw up the contract, and you can have your attorney look it over before you sign."

Sylvie was reluctant to tell him that she didn't have an attorney, so matter-of-fact was Chase in his announcement—as if everybody in the world kept a lawyer on retainer all the time. It occurred to her again what vastly differing life-styles they led. He was a man who was wildly successful in the cutthroat world of business, a man who seemed to have limitless funds and opportunities, a man who was completely in command of his destiny. His was a definite A-type personality, displaying all the characteristics of someone who took charge of a situation without being asked, who never questioned his own judgment, who worked from sunup to sundown to make sure the job was done right.

She, on the other hand, acted compulsively and spontaneously much of the time—her reasoning often based on nothing more than whimsy or intuition at that—and until deciding she wanted a baby, had seldom given much thought to where the future might take her. Certainly she was responsible enough—she was actively cultivating a decent savings account, lived within a monthly budget and had modest needs—but she didn't want to be the kind of person whose responsibilities extended beyond her own immediate experience. And having untold, very heavy responsibilities was something upon which Chase clearly thrived.

They simply came from and existed in two entirely different worlds. It was something that should comfort her, she tried to tell herself, something that should reinforce the fact that Chase would want no part of her life once he had completed the task she'd asked him to perform. Unfortunately, faced with their obvious differences and incompatibility, Sylvie found herself suddenly wondering if her maternity plan was such a good one after all.

"Sylvie?" she heard him ask, the mention of her name bringing her out of her reverie.

"What?" she replied, realizing he had been speaking at length and she had heard not a word of what he'd said. "I'm sorry, I wasn't listening. I was thinking about something else."

She wasn't sure, but she thought he paused for just the tiniest moment before asking, "What were you thinking about?"

She shook her head. "Nothing. Nothing important. What was it you were saying?"

He seemed to want to hedge. "I was talking about... What I was leading up to was... We haven't really..."

He ceased abruptly and looked away, focusing his attention on the wineglass on the table before him. Sylvie watched as he ran his finger casually along the lip of the glass, and for some reason her heart began to trip-hammer behind her rib cage. The circular motion of his hand was slow, methodical and hypnotic. Suddenly all she could think about was how his fingers would feel rotating in the same way over her bare skin. She closed her eyes and swallowed hard and tried to pay attention to what he was saying.

After collecting his thoughts for a moment, Chase began to speak again. "What I was wondering about... What I mean is..." He sighed deeply and, even without seeing him, she could tell he was growing impatient with himself. "Oh, hell," he muttered. "What I'm trying to say is that we haven't exactly discussed a...a *schedule,* if you know what I mean."

Sylvie's eyes fluttered open to find him gazing at her intently, and she fought back an urge that rose up out of nowhere—the urge to reach over and touch his face. "Schedule?" she asked, puzzled.

He nodded. "Last week you mentioned that you wanted a baby for Christmas. That you'd be..." His voice quieted noticeably as he continued, "You know... ovulating... in two weeks. I'm just wondering if that means..."

She nodded quickly to spare him having to speak the words she was suddenly frightened to hear. "Uh-huh. Um, I'd want you to... to... I'd want us to make love about a week from this Thursday. I've got one of those kits. One of those ovulation kits? You know, the kind that tells you exactly the right time to..." She cleared her throat discreetly. "Anyway, they're supposed to be pretty accurate."

"So what does that mean?" he asked. "That we get together Thursday night and—"

"How about if I call you?" she interrupted.

"Call me?"

"Yeah. It might not be Thursday exactly. It could be Friday or even Saturday. I could call you and let you know when I... when for sure I'll need you."

Chase frowned. He wasn't certain he liked the sound of that at all. Was he crazy? he asked himself yet again. What on earth had possessed him to agree to go along with this scheme of Sylvie's? What the hell did he think he was doing? For perhaps the hundredth time since saying yes that afternoon, he started to back out of the agreement.

Then he noticed once again the way her blue eyes grew darker in her anxiety, recalled the way she chewed her lower lip when she was thinking hard about something. Once again he remembered the way she had melted into him when he had kissed her that night beside her car. And for some reason he just couldn't get the words to voice his objection past his throat.

"You'll call me," he repeated blandly.

She nodded vigorously, her blond tresses bobbing with the gesture. He opened his mouth to say more, but quickly clamped it shut. This was ridiculous, he thought. What the two of them were planning was absolutely nuts. But deep down inside himself, he knew without a doubt that he was going to go through with it. His only fear at the moment was whether or not Sylvie was going to back out now.

"Well, it's getting late," he said without even looking at his watch. He swallowed the last of his wine and rose from the table, then tore the pertinent sheets of paper from the legal pad and folded them into quarters. "I really should get going."

"So soon?" Sylvie asked a little breathlessly as she stood beside him. He could tell, however, that she was relieved by his announcement.

"I skipped almost half a day of work today. I have a lot of catching up to do tonight."

He moved away from the dining-room table and went to retrieve his jacket and coat, then slipped wordlessly into both. He felt Sylvie watching him from behind and wished he knew what she was thinking. Was she wondering if she'd made a mistake? Did she consider him to be something less than human because he had so easily agreed to take a woman to bed in order to father a child for whom he would immediately relinquish all responsibility? Was she worried that maybe he wasn't such a great candidate for fatherhood after all?

For some reason Chase found himself wanting to drop to his knees and reassure her that he was a decent guy. He wanted to remind her that he'd built a thriving, successful company up from nothing, was extremely well respected among his colleagues and peers, had graduated with highest honors from Penn State University and had earned letters for baseball, track and hockey in high school. He wanted to tell her all about himself, about his family, his background, his hopes for the future. He wanted her to know that she could trust him.

And, he realized suddenly, he wanted her to know that he cared about her.

But he said nothing. Because he knew those were things Sylvie probably didn't want to know. And as much as he wanted to ask her about her own life experiences, her own hopes and dreams for the future, he decided he was probably better off not knowing.

They had made a deal, he reminded himself, stuffing the yellow pages of the unofficial contract into the breast pocket of his greatcoat. A deal by which he had agreed, for whatever reasons, a deal to which he would abide. He would make love to Sylvie Venner and give her a baby. And then he would stay out of her life for good.

When he turned around again, he saw her watching him closely, as if she had been entertaining thoughts similar to his own. He opened his mouth to tell her something, forgot what it was he was going to say, then moved across the room to stand before her. Without realizing what he was doing, he lowered his face to hers and kissed her, brushing his lips gently over hers in a whisper-soft caress. Then, when he realized what he had done, he immediately pulled away.

But not very far.

Because Sylvie had buried her fingers in the heavy fabric of his coat when he bent toward her, and she still clung to him fiercely, despite the chastity of his kiss. He was startled to find her gazing back at him with a longing unlike anything he'd ever witnessed in a woman before, a longing he knew mirrored the absolute need that burned deep within himself. And, unable to help himself, Chase bent toward her again.

This time when he kissed Sylvie it was anything but chaste. All the tension he'd been feeling since seeing her with her nephew that afternoon, all the loneliness of months of self-imposed solitude, all the simple basic need a man has for a woman came boiling to the surface, and he wrapped his arms around her, fully intending to never let her go.

When she lifted her hands and cupped the back of his neck to pull him closer, he tangled his fingers in her hair, glorying that the soft strands he encountered were every bit as silky as he had suspected they would be. He tilted her head to the side and kissed her more deeply, tasted her more fully. And for a few tempestuous moments he forgot all about the deal they had struck.

Until Sylvie pulled herself away from him with a ragged sigh, covering her mouth with one trembling hand as she ran the other nervously through her hair. She inhaled a single, deep, uneven breath, released it slowly, then crossed her arms over her abdomen.

"Uh, yeah, I think this is going to work out just fine," she said quietly, her voice sounding like a cannon shot in the otherwise silent room. "I, um, I guess I'll see you next week, then?"

Chase nodded, but didn't trust himself to speak for a moment.

Sylvie nodded in return. "Unless of course you come into Cosmo's between now and then," she added before clearing her throat anxiously.

Chase, too, inhaled a deep breath before responding. "Do you...do you want me to come into Cosmo's between now and then?"

"Sure, why not?" she said with a light chuckle that was clearly forced. She was trying to appear calm and unruffled, he noted, but she was doing a miserable job of faking it.

"Then I guess I'll see you tomorrow night as usual," he said, shoving his hands into his coat pockets.

"Good," she replied, her voice cracking on the word. She cleared her throat again and repeated, "Good."

"Tomorrow night," Chase said as he reached for the doorknob.

"Tomorrow night," she echoed as he opened the door. "Just like always."

He passed through without further comment, but paused out in the hallway. Slowly he pivoted to face her again. "Sylvie, I—" he began.

"Good night, Chase," she interrupted him, clearly unwilling to hear his explanation for what had just transpired between them. "And . . . thanks. For everything."

He flattened his lips into a tight line, but didn't argue. "Good night. I . . . I'll talk to you soon."

With one final, brief smile, Sylvie closed her front door quietly behind him, and he was left staring at the brass numbers of her address and the peephole beneath them. Chase had never felt more confused in his life than he did at that moment. And somehow, he was quite certain that this was just the beginning of his problems.

Four

Contrary to his assurances, Chase did not see Sylvie at Cosmo's the following night. Nor did he see her the night after that. Nor the night after that. In fact, so steadfast was his avoidance of the restaurant he seemed to have come to frequent more often than his own home that he was almost able to succeed in convincing himself that the whole episode with Sylvie and her desire for him to father her child was nothing more than a very strange dream. Almost.

Until he saw her again the following Wednesday.

He was just about to step into the conference room adjoining his office when his secretary, Lucille, buzzed him and offered the news that a Miss Sylvie Venner, who did not have an appointment, had expressed a desire to speak briefly with him. Chase glanced at his watch to discover that he was already five minutes late for a meeting with his associates and a *very* big prospective client, and shifting into businessman mode, asked Lucille to tell Miss Venner that he would telephone her at her home later this afternoon. Then, without waiting to hear what would happen next, he ducked quickly into the next room to attend to business.

Coward, he said to himself as he entered the conference room. *Running away from a beautiful woman whose sole desire is to have you make love to her.*

He closed the door behind himself and hastily rubbed his hand over his face, as if trying to erase any expression that might reveal the waywardness of his thoughts. Then he turned to the group of men and women who sat clustered in plum-colored chairs around the long, smoked-glass conference table, men and women who stared back at him expectantly.

"I'm sorry I'm late," he said, directing his apology first and foremost to the woman who sat directly opposite him at the other end of the table.

Ms. Gwendolyn Montgomery was a woman to be reckoned with, Chase reminded himself, a powerhouse in the development community who could potentially send millions of dollars worth of business his way. He'd heard through the grapevine that she was smart, attractive, extremely successful and quick to decide whether or not someone was worth her time. He knew he had his work cut out for him if he hoped to land her as a client.

Still, he thought, he was just as distinguished in his own field. He shouldn't have too much trouble amazing her with his architectural acumen, as long as nothing went phenomenally awry during the meeting. He was more than prepared for his presentation this morning. And really, what could possibly go wrong?

Almost involuntarily his gaze skittered away from the woman in question, and Chase found himself staring out the many-windowed wall of the conference room that looked into the reception area of his office. And there he saw another woman who commanded a piece of his future, a woman who appeared to be considerably less cool and collected than Ms. Gwendolyn Montgomery obviously was.

Sylvie Venner stood on the other side of the glass in the middle of the lobby, her rain-drenched trench coat flapping wildly over her dark, man-styled shirt, vest and trousers as she waved her arms frantically over her head in an effort to attract Chase's attention. Her hair, too, was wet, plastered about her face in wisps of dark blond, giving her the look of a fragile, helpless street urchin. When she saw that she had his attention, she smiled in relief and dropped her arms to her sides, evidently reassured that he would rush right out to see her.

Instead, Chase glanced quickly away again and addressed the group of people seated around the table. "We have a lot to go over this morning, and since I've already kept you waiting, why don't I just get right to the crux of the presentation?"

A rapid succession of *plink-plink-plink-plink-plink* sounds prevented him from continuing, however, because everyone in the room, including Chase, turned to discern the source of the noise. They all found Sylvie standing immediately on the other side of the conference-room windows, rapping the back of her hand against the glass, the rings on her fingers creating the annoying plinking sound. When she realized she had roused the interest of everyone in the room, she smiled anxiously, turning her hand around to wiggle her fingers in nervous greeting. Then she focused her attention on Chase, crooking her index finger at him in an effort to cajole him out of the room.

Chase tried to ignore her, making every effort to continue with his presentation. "Ms. Montgomery," he said, bringing the group's attention around to himself again. "I have some wonderful ideas for this project that I think you'll find more than ample for your needs. Some truly innovative suggestions that—"

Plink-plink-plink-plink-plink.

Again, everyone present turned back to the window. Sylvie's smile faltered this time, but she continued to meet Chase's gaze levelly. She lifted her other hand and jabbed a finger toward her wristwatch expressively. Everyone else in the room turned to gaze at Chase.

Chase looked at Ms. Montgomery and went on, "Truly innovative suggestions that I'm sure you're going to consider—"

Plink-plink-plink-plink-plink.

Chase sighed in exasperation and tried to take heart in the fact that this time only a handful of his colleagues turned to look at Sylvie. She continued to point at her watch, but her expression became more insistent, more anxious. Those who were still interested turned back to Chase, who lifted his shoulders in a shrug. Sylvie rolled her eyes heavenward, as if in a silent plea for patience. Then she silently mouthed something Chase couldn't quite make out. When he shook his head in confusion again, she slowly formed the words once more. This time he had no trouble translating.

The words she so theatrically mouthed were *I'm ov-u-la-ting.*

His eyes widened in shock and he looked at his guests again, hoping no one else present had deciphered what he had just figured out himself. Thankfully, everyone else appeared to have tired of the exchange. Again, he looked out at Sylvie, who continued to poke a finger at her watch. *Now,* she said silently before gesturing with her arms that he'd better hurry up.

"Uh, I'm really sorry," he said to the group. "Excuse me for a moment, will you...?" Without awaiting a reply, he bolted to the conference-room door and sped through it.

"What the hell are you doing here?" he demanded of Sylvie in a rough whisper, looking all around to be sure no one overheard their conversation.

"What do you think I'm doing here?" she countered just as frantically. She lowered her own voice. "I'm ovulating. Now. As we speak. You have to make love to me."

"Now?" he echoed.

"Well," she hedged, "according to the kit instructions, when the test comes back positive—and it turned as pink as the Easter Bunny's nose this morning—ovulation will occur sometime within the next twenty-four hours. But it could be happening now," she hastened to add.

"But you said it wouldn't happen until tomorrow. Or Friday. Or even Saturday. Couldn't we do this Saturday? I'm in the middle of something very—"

"So my timing was off," she interrupted him. "I've been a little anxious for the past couple of weeks. That can throw a woman's cycle off sometimes."

"But—"

"No buts," she told him. "We have to make love."

"Now?" he asked again.

"Now."

"Here?"

Sylvie rolled her eyes again. "Of course not *here*." She, too, glanced furtively around to be certain the two of them were not overheard. Then, with an uneasy smile, she announced, "I, uh, I got us a room. At the Four Seasons."

Chase's eyebrows shot up at that. "Are you serious?"

"Of course I'm serious. It's a wonderful hotel—beautiful and romantic. And it's only a couple of blocks away. I thought it would be the perfect atmosphere for...you know."

"Sylvie, I—"

"So you have to hurry. Once I drop that egg, we're talking about a window of opportunity here that only lasts about twelve hours."

He stared at her, completely befuddled, trying to convince himself that he must be dreaming. Unfortunately, the situation was simply too bizarre for him to have been conjuring it up in his unconscious mind.

"I can't leave right now," he finally told her. "I'm in the middle of a very important meeting."

A drop of rainwater fell from a loose strand of Sylvie's bangs and trickled down her cheek like a tear. "But what about *our* meeting?" she asked quietly. "That's very important, too."

"I know, but—"

"You promised, Chase. And I have a contract," she reminded him, pulling herself into what he was certain she considered a very imposing posture. With her rain-soaked hair and clothing, however, she succeeded in presenting herself as little more than a watered-down, helpless waif. And for some reason he suddenly wanted very badly to kiss her.

She stuffed her hand into the inside breast pocket of her coat and extracted the document in question. "See? It has both our signatures now. It's legal and binding."

That stupid contract, he thought. That was something else he couldn't believe he'd done—signed that damned thing. His attorney had called him every kind of fool when Chase had brought the handwritten sheets of yellow paper in for formalization. In fact, the other man had gone on for nearly an hour in an effort to make Chase see how many things could go wrong with the arrangement. And Chase hadn't been able to contradict his friend and adviser at all. But he'd still had him draw up the necessary papers. And then, calling himself an idiot even as he'd performed the task, Chase had signed his name on the dotted line and sent the contract via courier to Sylvie.

"All right," he finally relented, noting how her wet, spiky lashes made her eyes seem even bigger, even bluer, somehow. "I'll meet you at the Four Seasons in two hours."

Her expression fell. "But—"

"Surely two hours isn't going to make any difference, Sylvie." He lifted his hands to cup her shoulders, giving them an affectionate squeeze. Then, when he realized that the two of them were still the center of attention among virtually everyone in the office and conference room, he immediately dropped his hands back down to his sides.

"Maybe not," she agreed reluctantly.

"Besides," he added, "it will give you a little more time to think about this. To be sure it's what you want to do."

"Oh, it's definitely what I want to do," she told him vehemently. Her expression turned thoughtful as she added, "But something tells me you might be having second thoughts."

"No, no," he lied. "I'm perfectly willing to make . . . to make good on our agreement. But…" He looked back over his shoulder and into the conference room where he knew he was fast losing what might be the most important client of his career. "But this really is a very important meeting."

Sylvie looked past him, and he could tell her gaze settled at once on the stunning brunette who was Gwendolyn Montgomery. He wasn't sure, but he thought she deflated a little when she noted the other woman's presence. "Yeah, I bet it's important," she said.

"Two hours," Chase told her, holding up his hand to display the same number of fingers, as if illustrating his assurance to a child. "I'll see you in two hours."

Sylvie folded up the contract and tucked it back into her pocket, then swept her wet hair back from her face.

"Okay," she agreed. She reached into a different pocket and removed something else, an item small enough to hide in the palm of her hand and which she passed to Chase with another furtive glance around. "Here's a key to our room," she whispered. "Two hours. I'll be waiting."

He closed his fingers over the plastic key card, feeling like some kind of amateur secret agent in a truly bad spy thriller. "Thanks, Mata Hari," he mumbled under his breath. "Is there some special knock or secret handshake I should know about, too?"

"No," she replied with a shaky smile. "Just don't keep me waiting."

And with that she spun around and left his office without looking back. Chase watched her leave with a mixture of trepidation and desire, wondering all the while what had come over him the past couple of weeks. He wasn't behaving like himself at all. What had happened to the no-nonsense, height-of-efficiency, thoroughly-wrapped-up-in-his-company businessman he used to be? Lately he was jeopardizing professional relations, acting on impulse and lacking all sense of planning and forethought. Instead of being in control of his destiny he'd let fate come smack him right upside the head while he wasn't looking. And he was still reeling from the blow.

What was really crazy, though, Chase thought as he pocketed the room key and spun around toward the conference room again, was that he was actually kind of enjoying himself in his newfound state of chaos.

When he entered the conference room again, his guests and colleagues were watching him with a different kind of anticipation than they had seemed to feel before.

"My apologies for the delay," Chase said with a wistful smile he couldn't quite tamp down. He turned toward a nearby easel, pushed back the first page to reveal elaborate plans for a suburban fashion mall, and continued with his presentation.

She was crazy. She was absolutely nuts. She had done some truly odd things in her life, but asking a man she hardly knew to make love to her just so that she could have a baby was, without question, the most phenomenally bizarre. Yet, try as she might to talk herself out of what she was about to do, Sylvie found instead that she was actually looking forward to her afternoon with Chase Buchanan. And not, she was surprised to discover, exclusively because he was going to give her a child.

As she stared out the hotel-room window at the rainy street below, she remembered her doctor's words again, the ones that had pretty much forced her to make such a quick and drastic decision. If she was going to have a baby, Dr. Madison had told her, it had better be now.

How strange that she would find herself in this predicament—Sylvie Venner, who had spent her high school and college years touting the glory of the women's movement and the utter freedom to choose that such a social change brought with it. At sixteen, twenty-one, even as recently as twenty-nine years of age, she had been certain she would choose to remain single and child free forever. She'd had no interest in nor need of either men or the pitter-patter of little feet in her life, had been perfectly content with her own company. And she could conceive of nothing that would ever change her mind.

Until she'd met Simon, she thought, recalling her nephew. And until she'd been offered unequivocal evidence from her doctor that child free was exactly how she would remain for the rest of her life unless she did something to change that right away. Suddenly *choice,* that glorious concept that had always been her anthem, had taken on a new meaning. Because suddenly her choices in the area of motherhood were drastically reduced.

She'd had to think hard and fast about the question of maternity. For the first time in her life she had honestly, seriously, ponderously considered what it would mean to remain single and alone until the day she died. Sylvie's parents were gone now. Her sister was married and had started a family of her own. And her older brother, Carver, another firm believer in living life to its most solitary, spent almost all of his time traveling and out of touch. So where did that leave Sylvie in fifty or sixty years?

Alone, she had finally come to realize. And for the first time, the prospect of independent solitude didn't hold nearly as much appeal to her as it once had. Little by little Sylvie had decided that maybe, just maybe, solitude wasn't all it was cracked up to be. Independence came with a price tag, she had come to realize. And loneliness was a very high price to pay.

Ultimately deciding she didn't want to be alone for the long run, she'd made a choice. She'd chosen to become a mother. And seeing as she was looking at a severely limited amount of time left with which to pursue that choice, she'd made another one right on the heels of it.

She'd chosen not to wait around to fall in love with some guy.

Because guys, Sylvie knew, were nothing at all like children. Okay, actually they were very much like children, she'd amended quickly, but not in one extremely important aspect. Children, as long as you loved them and respected them and stuck by them, remained steadfastly devoted to you. Men, on the other hand, would dump you the minute something more interesting walked through the door.

A child, yes, she'd finally decided. A man, never.

Now as she turned to consider the plush, expensive hotel suite that she was really in no position to afford, Sylvie reaffirmed her decision. What she was doing was the right thing. If she missed this opportunity with Chase, she might never have another one.

As if thinking about him conjured him up, a quick, deliberate series of raps at the door alerted her to his arrival. Sylvie inhaled a deep breath, counted to ten and released it slowly. She surveyed the room one final time to be certain everything was in order.

The suite was filled with the fragrant perfume of a huge bouquet of exotic flowers and the mellow strains of some unidentifiable but undeniably romantic music she'd discovered on the in-room radio. The refreshment she'd ordered from room service had arrived only moments ago, and the champagne was chilling nicely in a sweaty silver ice bucket near an assortment of fruits, cheeses and breads. She'd turned down one corner of the king-size bed—just

enough to remind them both of the reason for their afternoon tryst—and smoothed the crisp white sheet and pillow
free of wrinkles.

Everything was ready, she thought. Everything necessary
for the perfect romantic rendezvous was here. Everything
except one thing. With a final deep breath she strode deliberately across the room to curl her fingers gingerly over the
doorknob, then twisted it to the right and pulled.

Five

Chase was there, his dark power suit now partially hidden beneath a rain-spattered trench coat. One hand dangled a wet umbrella at his side. The other cradled a single yellow rose. Sylvie smiled, trying to quell the trembling that wanted to shake her from her head to her toes.

"Hi," she said softly.

"Hi," he replied.

"Glad you could make it."

"Wouldn't miss it for the world."

They continued to stare at each other for some moments without moving, until Chase extended the rose toward her.

"I guess red would have been more appropriate for the occasion," he said as she closed her fingers around the long stem. "But somehow, you seem more a yellow rose type to me."

She lifted the perfect bloom to her nose and inhaled deeply, reveling in the tangy-sweet scent. "It's beautiful," she told him softly. "And yellow roses are my favorite. Thank you."

He looked at her for another long moment without speaking, then finally asked, "Can I . . . can I come in?"

"Oh, of course," she said, stepping quickly backward to allow him entry.

The moment he was in the room she closed the door behind him with a quiet *click*. He shrugged out of his trench coat and went to the closet to hang it up beside hers. The image hit Sylvie strangely—two raincoats hanging side by side the sole occupants of a hotel-suite closet. When Chase turned to face her, she could tell by his expression that his thoughts mirrored her own.

She fingered the delicate bloom of the rose softly and wondered what she should do next. She'd never been in the position of seducer before. Just what exactly was the protocol in a situation like this?

"Would you like some champagne?" she asked.

He seemed relieved by the question, and she wondered if he had been thinking she would simply order him to strip off his clothes and get into bed that instant.

"I'd love some," he told her, moving toward the table. "But please, allow me."

With quick, deft fingers he unwrapped the foil from the bottle's head and removed the cage covering the cork. Then, with a crisp *pop,* he thumbed the cork out, chuckling as he caught the initial stream of effervescent wine in a linen towel. It occurred to Sylvie then that he must have opened a lot of champagne in his time, so expertly had he performed the function. And seeing as how *she* was the one who was a bartender here, she couldn't help but wonder, too, how many occasions like this one he'd had to celebrate in the past.

It didn't matter, she told herself. If he'd been with other women in the past—if he would be with other women in the future—it simply didn't matter. She wasn't exactly a blushing virgin herself, and she certainly wasn't expecting him to hang around and be a part of her future. For some reason, though, the thought of Chase Buchanan with other women didn't sit well with her at all.

He plucked two strawberries from a silver bowl on the tray and dropped one into each of the long-stemmed crystal flutes before filling them with champagne. Then he settled the bottle back into its icy resting place, lifted a glass into each hand and came to join Sylvie near the bed.

"You do know your champagne," he said of the Dom Pérignon.

She shrugged as she took the glass he extended toward her. "Hey, I am a bartender after all."

They sipped their wine in silence, each gazing at the other as if sizing up the situation and wondering what to do next. Sylvie had never been nervous around a man before. She'd never taken one seriously enough to become anxious about him. But Chase made her feel more than nervous. He made her feel something she couldn't recall ever feeling before. Something wild and giddy and utterly exciting. Something she wasn't sure she should be feeling when the man in question was little more than a springboard for her future happiness.

"Nice music," he finally said, indicating the wail of a saxophone that seemed to surround them with a plaintive invitation. "Coltrane. Good stuff. Are you a big fan of jazz?"

Sylvie shook her head as she sipped her champagne. The cool, bubbly liquid felt good against her suddenly parched throat. "No. I mean, I really don't know anything about jazz. Even though Cosmo plays it at the restaurant all the time, I've never really paid much attention to it."

"What kind of music do you like?"

"Alternative, mostly."

"What's that?"

"Oh, you know, Spin Doctors, Gin Blossoms, Lemonheads, Smashing Pumpkins, Counting Crows…." Her voice trailed off as a look of confusion clouded his face, and she smiled. "I think they called it New Wave way back when you were young."

He had been lifting his glass to his lips again, but stilled the motion at her playful jab. He frowned at her. "Excuse me? I happen to think I'm still young. Certainly I'm not ready for the nursing home yet."

She chuckled. "Oh, I'm only kidding, Chase. Geez. I hope our baby gets *my* sense of humor."

The sudden mention of why they were there sobered them both immediately.

"*Our* baby?" Chase repeated in a deceptively quiet voice.

Had she really said that? Sylvie asked herself. "I mean *my* baby," she corrected herself immediately. "I hope *my* baby gets my sense of humor."

He nodded and sipped his drink, and she wished she knew what he was thinking.

"This is your show, Sylvie," he said when he had swallowed. "So what do we do next?"

Good question, she thought. "I, um...I don't know. I guess we could...I mean, I could...Or...or *you* could if you want. I'm really not particular."

"I could what?"

She parted her lips to exhale a shaky breath, but instead all that emerged was a quietly uttered question, two simple little words that said more than enough. "Kiss me?"

Without hesitation Chase set his glass on the bedside table, removed the rose and her own glass from her now-numb hands to place them beside his, then pulled her resolutely into his arms. Before Sylvie had a chance to even think about what was happening, he touched his mouth to hers, brushing her lips gently with his in a sweet, simple, inquisitive caress. Her eyelids fluttered closed, her fingers curled into the lapels of his suit jacket and her body melted into his. For just a split second he pulled away from her, then he kissed her again, in exactly the same way. All Sylvie could think about was that she'd never felt quite so...so cherished...before.

She wasn't sure how long they remained embraced that way, exchanging almost harmless touches and tentative caresses. Then what had begun as a kind of subtle exploration gradually grew bolder. Sylvie's fingers seemed to travel of their own free will from Chase's lapel to his neck, then to his face, then to his hair. Blindly she gauged every surface she encountered, from the smooth fabric of his shirt to the warm roughness of his jaw to the silky softness of the dark tresses twining around her fingers. The scent of him surrounded her, a fragrance at once spicy and sweet, something she'd never quite detected on a man before.

And as she slowly investigated more of Chase, he began an experimental examination of his own. As his kisses lengthened and grew more intense, she felt his hands begin to glide over her. He had bunched a fistful of her hair at her nape when he first embraced her, but now released it and dropped his hands to her shoulders. He pulled her closer, splaying his fingers open over her back, sliding them oh-so-casually down her spine only to stop at the small of her back as if fearful of a more intimate touch.

Sylvie pulled back from him only far enough to study his face, and was relieved at what she saw there. He was as nervous about this as she was, she realized. As nervous as she... and as eager for it to continue to its obvious conclusion.

"Are you scared?" she asked him quietly.

He nodded slowly. "Yes. Yes, I am."

She smiled. "Me, too."

"Do you want to stop? Do you want to change your mind about this?"

She shook her head. "No, I..." She groped for words that might begin to explain her feelings, but none seemed appropriate. Finally she told him, "This feels good, Chase. This feels right somehow. I think it's a sign."

"A sign?" he echoed, tangling his fingers in her hair once again. He dipped his head and kissed her temple softly, then pressed his forehead against hers. "A sign of what?"

She closed her eyes at the shivery sensation that wound through her when he traced her jaw with his thumb. "I think we're going to be successful today. I think we're... I think we're going to make a baby today."

He pulled his head away from hers when she voiced her certainty and gazed at her with solemn green eyes. For a moment she feared he was going to pull away from her completely and call the whole thing off. Then he smiled, a slow, languid, easy kind of smile, and she knew everything was going to be all right.

"You're sure?" he asked her quietly, hooking his hands at the small of her back again. "You're absolutely certain this is what you want to do?"

"Yes," she told him. "It's exactly what I want to do."

Chase studied the woman in his arms closely, wishing with all his heart that he had the nerve to ask her why she wanted to do this. Was it only because she wanted a baby? he asked himself instead. Or could there possibly be some part of her—even some tiny part way deep down inside—that might, just maybe, want him a little bit, too?

He was probably better off not voicing the question, he decided. He probably didn't want to hear her answer. So instead he kissed her again, reveling in the contentment and satisfaction that came with holding another human being so close after so long. And he tried not to remember how much he had come to care for her over the years.

As Sylvie lifted her hands to struggle fretfully with the tie knotted at his throat, Chase began to work more methodically at the buttons on her man-style vest. It fell to the floor just as she tugged the length of silk from beneath his collar. Their gazes never parted as each started unfastening the buttons of the other's shirt, but when Chase glimpsed a flash of black lace beneath Sylvie's sapphire blue blouse, he couldn't help but take notice.

He suddenly began to hasten his fingers almost feverishly in their task, pulling her shirttail free of her dark trousers before reaching for the button and zipper at her waist, impatient to discover the true nature of her underthings. But Sylvie's hand curled over his and moved it shyly away.

"Wait," she said, two bright spots of pink staining her cheeks. Her eyes sparkled with something Chase wasn't quite able to identify. "Let me."

She, too, had freed his shirt from his trousers, and had tangled her fingers in the black hair that was scattered across his chest and down the entire length of his torso. Like Sylvie, he stood with his shirt gaping open, but where he was essentially naked beneath the rest of his clothing, Sylvie was dressed in something more. Something that he found very...intriguing.

Her gaze never leaving his, she lifted her hands to her waistband and unfastened her trousers, skimming them off over long legs encased in smoky black silk. Then she shrugged out of her shirt, tossing it toward a nearby chair without even looking to see if the garment hit its target. Chase swallowed hard and was almost afraid to look down, but his curiosity, along with a few other things, got the better of him.

Sylvie Venner—a woman who until recently he'd never seen dressed in anything other than her shapeless bartender's garb—now stood before him wearing a little black scrap of nothing that included lacy garters, black stockings and black high heels. His mouth dropped open in astonishment. Never, not in a million years, would he have guessed that she wore such things under the masculine-looking clothing she seemed to favor. And never would he have guessed that she was so exquisitely formed.

"Uh..." he said eloquently.

He looked at her face long enough to see her tremulous smile falter, but his gaze was pulled irresistibly back to her attire. "Uh..." he repeated.

"You don't like it?" Sylvie asked, her voice edged with disappointment. "But I thought this was the kind of thing men liked to see women wear for a...you know...a, um..." She lowered her voice to a whisper. "A sexual encounter."

"Uh..."

"I thought it might, shall we say, put you in the mood."

He wanted to tell her he'd been in the mood ever since she'd asked him to be the one to father her child. Before then, even. He'd probably been wanting to make love to Sylvie Venner since the night he first walked into Cosmo's and saw her standing behind the bar.

"Sylvie, I..." He continued to study her little outfit as he ran his hands restlessly through his hair, rubbed his palms over the back of his scalp and hooked his fingers at the nape of his neck. He sighed deeply, not sure he trusted his own voice. "I don't think you have to worry about me being in the mood. You, uh..." His gaze finally rose to link with hers again. "Trust me—it's just not an issue," he concluded.

She smiled again, that shy smile that made him want to wrap his arms around her and never let her go. Then he took the single step necessary to bring his body flush with hers and dropped his hands to her bare shoulders. She flattened her palms against his chest, skimming her hands up and over his shoulders to push his shirt away. It fluttered to the ground unnoticed, and she moved her hands lower, to his belt.

Chase sucked in a ragged breath at the brush of her nimble fingers, fingers that seemed to want to linger at his waist. When he bent to kiss her again, she deftly unhooked his belt and lowered the zipper of his trousers. Slowly, leisurely, letting the mellow music that still surrounded them be his guide, he danced her backward to the bed, his kiss growing deeper and more intimate as he moved. Sylvie kissed him back with equal fire, circling his waist with her hands until her fingers splayed open over his bare back.

And then Chase completely forgot why he was there. He forgot all about Sylvie's proposal, all about the baby she wanted him to father for her, all about the contract they had signed. Instead, only one thought materialized from the host of feverish ideas muddling his brain—the realization that there was something he wanted, too. He wanted Sylvie Venner. And not just for one afternoon.

And then even that thought was gone. Because Sylvie had successfully divested him of the remainder of his clothing, and he could feel her pressing against him from head to toe. Slowly, deliberately, leisurely, he pushed himself more insistently against her, urging her back toward the bed. Together they performed an uneven dance of desire and exploration, until the feel of smooth, crisp sheets somehow came to envelop them.

Warm, silky skin and cool, soft lace seemed to fuse, and Chase was never quite certain where Sylvie ended and he began. He tangled his fingers in a black ribbon wound into a discreet bow between her breasts and unraveled it, dipping his fingers inside to explore the warm valley he encountered beneath. As his hand ventured downward, the black lace seemed to want to follow, until it bunched below one breast as if in invitation.

His mouth followed the path his fingers had traveled, and he pressed his lips to the stiff pink flesh that beckoned him. Sylvie moaned low when he tasted her, burying her fingers in his hair when he drew her more fully into his mouth. As he tongued and suckled her urgently, he cupped her other breast and pressed his fingers against her, pushing the fabric away from her tender flesh and down farther still. He had never known anything could be so soft, so tender, so inviting. And he'd never been more aroused in his life.

Sylvie, too, had lost herself in a world of wild sensations. Her head rolled back on the pillow when Chase laved her breast with his tongue, but when she felt his fingers dipping lower, into her navel and beyond, she snapped her head forward again. He was exploring parts of her she'd seldom thought about herself, and making quite a thorough search of them. She gasped when he dipped his hand lower still, skimming the black lace away from her body completely, touching her more intimately than she had ever been touched before.

"Oh, Chase," she whispered. "What are you doing to me?"

She heard the low rumble of satisfied laughter, then he turned his head so that he could look at her face. "Hey, I'm just getting warmed up," he told her with a wicked smile.

Another flick of his hand caused her eyes to roll backward, and she groaned again. She, too, had forgotten the true reason for their tryst long ago, and now could only ponder the wild sensations that Chase's ministrations had set free. Warmed up? she repeated to herself dazedly. Oh, boy....

He tugged on the lacy black get-up she had purchased just that morning for just this occasion, pulling it off in its entirety until she lay on the bed as naked as he. And then he came to her again, kissed her temple, her neck, her breast, her belly, then ducked his head lower to languidly give her a gift like none she'd ever received before. She twisted her fingers in his hair and in the sheet beneath her, turning her head into the pillow to stifle a cry of surrender.

By the time Chase moved to settle his big body atop hers, bracing himself on his elbows as he buried his fists in her hair, Sylvie was trembling with her need for him. She lifted her arms almost weakly to circle his neck, then pulled him down to kiss him, luxuriating in the hard, heavy feel of his body against hers.

"Chase," she whispered against his mouth. "I need you. Badly. Now."

"Now?" he repeated with a smile, parroting the question he had asked her in his office that morning.

"Right now," she insisted.

She raked her fingers down his long, muscular torso until she encountered the part of him she so desired, cradling him fully in her palm. He squeezed his eyes closed and gasped out something she didn't understand, then tried to move away from her. Instinctively she tightened her grip, something that made him thrash wildly before stilling himself completely. He seemed to her a caged animal then, one who's tasted what it is to be utterly free, and who's nearly—but not quite—forgotten how spectacular that freedom can be. When his eyes met hers, they burned like a sleek, green flame. He placed his hand over hers.

"It's been a while for me," he whispered raggedly. "I'm not sure how much longer I can last."

She moved her head slowly from side to side on the pillow, wanting to tell him so much, but not entirely certain she had the strength to speak that many words. Finally she decided on just three. "Love me, Chase," she whispered, brushing her fingers over him again. "That's all I need or want."

He closed his eyes tight and lowered himself slowly, letting her be his guide. A vast, white heat enveloped him as he entered her, shattering in its intensity, blinding in its incandescence. With every deep stroke his body made, he felt himself pulled more insistently toward it, felt Sylvie going with him as he hurtled toward its center. And the closer he moved to the center the more he burned, until all he could sense was their two bodies melting together. He cried out her name in a ragged whisper as he reached his peak, then collapsed into her arms.

For long moments he could only feel. Could only marvel at the magnitude of their culmination. Then gradually he struggled back into coherence, only to find himself still surrounded by Sylvie. She seemed to be everywhere. Seemed to have seeped into every pore in his body, every cell in his brain, every beat of his heart.

The next thing he knew, she was lying atop him. He lay on his back, cradling her in his arms, gasping for breath and groping for some semblance of normal thought. He twisted her hair in his fingers and ran his palm idly over the slick, wet surface of her back. She had tucked her head into the curve beneath his chin and buried her fingers in the dense hair on his chest. He heard her sigh—a sound that was at once full of contentment and longing.

"Are you okay?" he managed to ask her.

He felt her nod, a slow, satisfied gesture. "Oh, yes," she murmured, tilting her head back to study him. "I feel wonderful. Are you okay?"

Okay probably wasn't the most descriptive word he could use to identify the massive confusion pummeling his brain at the moment, Chase thought, but the rest of his body felt better than it ever had before. Reluctantly he nodded his head, too. "Yeah," he said, not quite convinced his answer was the truth. "Yeah, I'm okay, too."

She snuggled closer to him, and he could have sworn their two hearts were beating in exactly the same rhythm. He pulled her nearer and kissed the crown of her head, then was amazed to discover that he wanted her again. More desperately than ever. And right away.

"Uh, Sylvie," he said.

"Hmm?"

"You, um, you don't work on Wednesdays, do you?"

"Mmm, hmm."

"You don't have to baby-sit for your nephew today?"

"I called Livy this morning after the test came back positive and told her I wouldn't be available today. She took Simon to work with her. There's a day-care center at the hospital."

"I see."

"Why?"

Chase nibbled his lip thoughtfully. "So that means you really don't have anywhere you have to be this afternoon."

Sylvie looked up at him once more and smiled. "No...." she said, her voice trailing off when she realized where his thoughts were headed.

"You know," he began again, rubbing the pad of his thumb slowly up and down the length of her spine. She shivered at the heat that shot through her. "It would be a real shame to waste a beautiful room like this. I mean, we still have a bottle of champagne to drink, and all that food over there looks delicious."

"Yes...."

"And I don't think there's any pressing reason for me to hurry back to the office."

"Oh?"

"No. I don't see why we couldn't just spend the rest of the afternoon together. Doing...whatever."

Sylvie smiled and sat up in bed, wrapping the sheet around her like a sari. She knew she should tell Chase that it wasn't necessary for them to try again, that making love twice in a very short period of time was in no way conducive to reproduction. Clinically speaking, she should tell him, when two people were expressly trying to make a baby, it was best for the man to wait another forty-eight hours before they tried again. She could have quoted medical statistics and scientific data that would have illustrated most convincingly that there was really no point in their making love a second time that afternoon.

Then she remembered that one crystal-clear moment when Chase had taken her to a place she'd never been before. She recalled how badly she had wanted to stay in that place with him forever. And instead, Sylvie found herself replying, "Oh, what the heck. One more time couldn't hurt."

Six

Sylvie was anxious as she worked her shift at Cosmo's the following night. Her gaze kept creeping toward her wristwatch, and the closer the hour hand came to the number seven, the more erratically her heart began to pound. Chase generally arrived for dinner between seven and seven-thirty, and for the first time she could ever remember, she was anticipating his arrival—anticipating it with both dread and a thrill of excitement. But mostly, she realized, she was anticipating it with worry.

She recalled the previous afternoon's escapades with a hot face and trembling hands. The things they'd done to each other, she marveled again. The way Chase had made her feel. What on earth had she been thinking when she'd told him they could go back to their usual routine once he'd completed the mission she'd asked him to undertake? How could she have thought for a moment that nothing would change between them after a shared experience like... like... like *that?*

The moment he walked into the bar, she knew she would collapse into a heap of blathering idiocy. She had no idea what to say to him, had no idea how to act. It wasn't that she was embarrassed by or ashamed of what they had done together. She was just . . . amazed. Amazed at what had happened when he'd made love to her. Amazed at the way she had felt. Why, that third time they'd come together she'd been *that* close to crying out that she loved him. And the way he had kissed her when it had finally come time to say goodbye, a kiss full of promise and a secret kind of knowledge. . . . Sylvie sighed wistfully in spite of herself.

She shook her head and turned to look longingly at the rows of liquor lined up behind her. Boy, a healthy shot of something ninety proof would do wonders to settle her nerves, she thought. But that was out of the question. She had very good reason to believe there might be a spark of life generating inside her this very instant. And she tried to focus on that concept instead of her troubling memories of Chase Buchanan. A baby, she reminded herself. That, and nothing more, was what yesterday afternoon had been about.

But when she glanced into the mirror behind the bottles of liquor and saw Chase approaching, she thoroughly forgot about that. Instead, an almost overwhelming wave of erotic memory swept over her, and she had to count to ten before she allowed herself to react to his presence. She took her time studying him as he approached the bar, noting the utter confidence with which he carried himself and the comfort he so clearly felt in his expensive dark suit. It was amazing really, she thought, that the two of them had ever hit it off at all, let alone generated the kind of explosive responses in each other that they had created the previous afternoon.

She watched as he seated himself at the bar, his gaze fastened to hers in the mirror's reflection. She knew she would have to turn and face him eventually, knew she was going to have to come up with something witty and clever to say that might ease the tension she could feel burning up the air between them. But for some reason her body refused to move in any way, and she remained glued steadfastly in place.

"Hello, Sylvie," Chase said, finally breaking the silence that had threatened to engulf her.

Somehow she forced her feet to pivot her body around, and she faced him with all the casual nonchalance she could fake. "Hi," she greeted him, amazed that the single syllable sounded so free of angst. She reached automatically for the brand of Scotch he preferred.

"No," he said, the word startling her. "I want something different tonight."

She was afraid to ask what, so she simply arched a brow in silent question.

"Champagne," he told her with a smile. "I'm celebrating. Bring me a whole bottle of whatever you like best."

She wanted to remind him that he already knew exactly what she liked best—and not just where champagne was concerned—but bit her lip to prevent herself from uttering the comment aloud. Instead she nodded and went to the wine cooler to extract a bottle of the same champagne they had enjoyed the day before. She called herself a fool for doing it, knowing she should avoid any reminder of their intimate encounter, but something inside her rebelled at the prospect of forgetting yesterday afternoon.

She could tell that Chase recognized the label immediately by the way he smiled at her, and his eyes never left hers as she extracted the cork from the bottle with a muffled *pop*. She pulled down a glass and filled it with effervescent gold, then pushed it across the bar toward him.

"Join me?" he asked as he lifted it in his hand.

She shook her head. "I'm working. Cosmo frowns on it."

"And you could be pregnant," he added quietly.

She felt her cheeks flush. "Well, it's still way too early to know that. I won't be able to tell for sure for a couple of weeks."

"But you think you are."

It was a statement, not a question, she realized. "I think I am," she said with a nod.

He smiled and lifted the glass to his lips.

"So, um, what are you celebrating tonight?" Sylvie asked, trying to sound breezy and neutral, at once hopeful and fearful that his response would include both of them.

He returned his glass to the bar and smiled again. "Today I signed the biggest client of my career."

Something cool and uncomfortable surrounded her heart, and she found it difficult to remember why she should be reassured by his answer. "Oh?"

Chase nodded. "She's going to bring enough business my way to keep me in contracts for the next five years. Probably longer."

Sylvie forced a smile. "That's great, Chase. That's..." She sighed fitfully. "Congratulations."

"Thanks."

"Was she the one at your very important meeting yesterday morning?"

"That's her. Gwendolyn Montgomery. She's a major player in the development game. Maybe you've heard of her?"

Sylvie shook her head. No, she'd never heard of Gwendolyn Montgomery before, but she recalled all too well the slender, cool-looking brunette with the piercing gray eyes—the one who had been wearing a dark power suit that rivaled Chase's, the one who had been looking over her shoulder at him as though he were a prize-winning dessert. Oh, yeah, she thought. No doubt that woman was going to be a very important *client* indeed.

"Nope, sorry," Sylvie said as she pushed the odd pang of jealousy away. "But I'm glad she's going to be, uh, helping you out." She reached for the order pad tucked into her apron pocket, then tugged a stub of pencil from behind her ear. "So, you want me to run over tonight's specials? Cosmo is especially proud of his quail this evening, but I had the pork medallions in wine sauce before my shift and they were really yummy. There's also a swordfish steak that's—"

"Sylvie."

Chase spoke her name as he had the afternoon before, in a way that was low and languid and very, very seductive. She couldn't bring herself to glance up at him, because she was afraid that if she did, she would find him looking at her as he had yesterday—with eyes that were full of something she had been afraid to identify. So instead, she tapped her pencil restlessly against the order pad, studying the two objects as if she intended to use them in the creation of a literary masterpiece.

"Yes?" she replied quietly.

"I'd really like to talk about something other than dinner."

"Oh? Like what?"

"Like us."

She finally did look up, but not directly at Chase. Gazing at the Boston ferns that surrounded a grand piano behind him, she asked, "Us? Why would you want to talk about us?"

He leaned a little to his right in an effort to place himself in her line of vision, but Sylvie obstinately refused to acknowledge him. She heard him sigh, a sound of resignation, then he moved back to his original position.

"I thought maybe after yesterday—" he began.

"What about yesterday?" she interrupted him, still striving for a carelessness she didn't feel.

"Sylvie, look at me."

She finally relented and did as he requested, immediately sorry for her surrender when her gaze met his. He was so handsome, she thought, wondering again why she had never really paid much attention to the fact before. Until a couple of weeks ago he'd been just another customer, albeit one with whom she shared a better-than-average relationship. She'd always enjoyed talking to him when he was just Mr. Buchanan, had found his career fascinating and had been flattered that he so often asked her advice about everything from his work to whether a woman would prefer candy or flowers for Valentine's Day.

They'd created a wonderful rapport with each other, a comfortable, very friendly rapport. And she couldn't help but worry that they'd managed to blow that with one afternoon's encounter.

"What?" she asked him.

His eyes never left hers as he said, "I think we need to talk about what happened yesterday."

"Why?"

She could see that he was disappointed in her reluctance to discuss their tryst. Nevertheless, he told her, "Because it's important."

She dropped her gaze to the pencil she twisted nervously between her fingers. "Of course it was important. You were fulfilling a contractual obligation."

When she looked at him again, his expression had changed from consideration to exasperation. "If you'll think back," he said, his voice losing the tone of tenderness it had held before, "I did a hell of a lot more than fulfill a contractual obligation. And if memory serves," he added pointedly, "so did you."

Sylvie blushed, feeling as if her body temperature suddenly rose by ten degrees. She didn't know why she was behaving this way, like some 'B' list client of his who simply wanted to thank him for a job well done. She only knew that for some reason she had to put some distance between herself and Chase Buchanan. Pronto. A big distance. And the only way she could think of to do that was to make light of what had happened between them. It should be taken lightly, she reminded herself. There had been nothing more to yesterday's encounter than what they had originally agreed. They had made a deal, and now that deal was fulfilled. Period. She'd be better off remembering that.

"Chase, all that happened between us yesterday is that you did me a favor."

"A *favor?*" he demanded, clearly outraged by the thought.

She nodded, tightening her grip on the pencil and pad she still held, praying with all her might that he couldn't see her hands trembling. "A favor for which I thank you enormously. I'm not sure I can ever repay you for your generosity—"

"My *generosity?*" he sputtered.

"But you agreed to...to perform a service for me."

His eyes widened in affront at the casual way she'd worded what had happened between them, and he opened his mouth to object again.

Sylvie held up her hand to stop him. "And you also agreed to something else," she said. "We both did. We agreed that after we...after we made love...then we would go back to things being exactly the same way they had been between us before. Before...all this...happened."

He eyed her warily, and a sudden sense of hopelessness settled over her. Before he could say anything else that would make the situation even more difficult, she placed the pad and pencil back in her apron pocket and spread her hands open, palm up, on the bar. It occurred to her that the gesture looked like one of surrender, and she sighed heavily before she continued.

"Chase, please," she said softly. "Don't. Don't turn yesterday into something it wasn't."

He studied her for a long moment before replying, and his voice was strained and angry sounding when he did. "Then tell me, Sylvie. Just exactly what *was* yesterday afternoon?"

She lifted her chin a fraction of an inch, hoping the posture would make her seem confident of her words, even if she was in no way convinced there was an iota of truth in her statement. "I needed a man—an extraordinary man—to father a child for me. You agreed to be that man, and you did what I asked you to do. That was all. And now that's the end of it. That's all there is to it. Now we go back to just being friends."

"You're willing to do that?" he asked. "You think you're *capable* of doing that?"

"Of course," she lied. "Why wouldn't I be?"

A muscle twitched slightly at the corner of his mouth. "And what if things didn't work out yesterday the way they're supposed to?" he asked evenly.

She swallowed hard, but met his gaze without flinching. "What do you mean?"

"What if you're not pregnant? What happens then?"

Her gaze skittered to the floor. "Then I guess we try again next month. That's what we decided, wasn't it? That's what we put in the contract."

When she looked up at him again, he shook his head vehemently, two times. "No, Sylvie. *You* try again. Contract or no, the next time, leave me out of it."

"But—"

His eyes flashed at her, but he lowered his voice when he said, "I must have been nuts when I told you I'd make love to you to give you a baby. I must have been completely out of my mind. I tried to convince myself that what you were asking me to do would create the perfect situation. That you'd get the baby you wanted and I'd have sex, something I definitely haven't been getting enough of lately, as evidenced by the phenomenally insane way I agreed to be your stud. But you know what's really crazy?''

She shook her head, unable to utter a single word in her own defense.

"What's really crazy is that after I agreed to do it, I actually started to think that maybe there was a chance that—''

He broke off abruptly and shook his head again, this time quickly, as if trying to clear it. "No, never mind what I started to think. Forget it. It isn't important. I really must be crazy if I thought..."

His last words were spoken so softly that Sylvie had to strain to hear them, and she instinctively knew he had meant the comment only for himself. Without another word he reached into his pocket for his wallet, tossed a handful of twenties onto the bar to cover the cost of the champagne he'd barely sampled, and pushed himself away from the bar.

Sylvie watched him leave, a swirl of turbulent emotions battering at her brain. Chase didn't look back once, and in fact seemed to have forgotten her the second he turned around. It was for the best, she told herself. Whatever she thought she might have felt yesterday, it was only the result of an unusually satisfying sexual encounter. She didn't love Chase Buchanan. He was a nice guy, and it had been awfully generous of him to perform the function she'd asked of him. But he wasn't a man for her. No man was for her.

She curled her fingers dispassionately around the neck of the champagne bottle and studied the label she already knew quite well. It was an expensive brand, one that people used only for celebrating the most important of life's special moments. Usually Sylvie loved the bubbly stuff. But at the moment she had absolutely no appetite for it. Tipping it slowly over the sink below the bar, she watched the shimmering gold contents spill out against the stainless steel, splashing in a cloud of white foam before dribbling down the drain.

And she wondered if Cosmo had any openings on the day shift.

* * *

Two weeks later Sylvie closed her eyes as she pulled the plastic stick out of the grayish solution in the test tube. She wasn't sure she wanted to know, was afraid of how crushed she would be if the tip of the wand was white instead of blue. She gripped the tiny stick between her thumb and index finger, lifted it to what she figured was pretty much eye level and forced herself to pry one eye open.

Blue. She distinctly saw the presence of blue.

She opened her other eye cautiously, not trusting one to do the job efficiently. The tip of the wand remained blue—dark blue, most definitely blue—even with both eyes open. She sucked in an incredulous breath and reached for the pregnancy kit instruction sheet to double-check her findings. "If the tip of the wand turns blue," she read, "this indicates a positive result, and you should consider yourself pregnant. See a doctor immediately for verification and to begin proper prenatal care."

"Oh, my gosh," she whispered, splaying her fingers open over her flat belly. Vaguely she felt the plastic wand go tumbling from her other hand onto the tile floor of her bathroom, but all she could do was stare at her reflection in the mirror over the sink. "Oh, my gosh," she repeated almost silently.

For a full five minutes she could only stand fixed in place, marveling at what had happened. She was pregnant. She was going to have a child. A giddy, almost overwhelming happiness swept over her, and she laughed—a trembling, nervous laugh, but one that was undeniably the result of joy. Sheer, utter, rapturous joy. Sylvie threw her arms around herself in an ecstatic hug. She couldn't remember another time in her life when she had been happier.

She had to tell Chase.

The thought erupted in her brain like a steam locomotive through a tunnel at full throttle. But why Chase Buchanan should be the first thing she considered was a mystery to her. He hadn't come back to Cosmo's for his usual dinner after leaving so angrily more than two weeks ago. And if he returned now, she would miss him, because she started working the day shift next week.

She already missed him, she realized. She'd been missing him for weeks. But she told herself it would be a mistake to try to contact him now. Hadn't she made it clear—to him and to herself—that he had no place in her life, or her child's? Hadn't she pointed out more than once that if she got pregnant, that would be the end of their obligation to each other? Hadn't she expressly insisted that what had occurred at the hotel had happened only because she wanted him to give her a child? And now that he'd given her a child, there was no reason for her to stay in touch, right?

Especially since a child was the last thing Chase wanted. Especially since he had neither the time nor the desire to include a family in his life. He had been as adamant in describing his contempt for children as she had been in avowing her love for them. There was absolutely no good reason that she should rush over to Chase's office to tell him the news. He'd probably recoil from the information. He'd probably recoil from her.

She bent to scoop up the plastic indicator from the floor and studied it again. It was even bluer now than it had been before. Chase Buchanan had fulfilled his contractual obligation to her, had given her the baby she had asked him to provide for her. She would be grateful to him for the rest of her life, every time she looked at the child who accompanied her on that journey. There was nothing wrong with telling him thank-you, was there?

She smiled and began to hum to herself, a song about going to the animal fair, about the birds and the beasts that were there. It was a song her mother had sung to her when she was just a little girl, and it made Sylvie laugh as she stepped into the shower.

Chase studied the blueprints spread open on his desk and tried to remember what he had been about to say to Gwen. She wasn't Ms. Montgomery anymore. She wasn't even Gwendolyn. Scarcely two weeks into the mall project, he thought with inexplicable annoyance, and, at her insistence, the two of them were already down to comfortable nicknames.

Instead of looking at the elaborate series of lines and circles that crisscrossed and dotted the blueprints, however, Chase was surveying the slender hand that had settled next to his on the page. The smooth skin, tanned to a toasty golden perfection even at the close of winter, suggested that Gwen had either recently returned from a tropical vacation or made regular visits to the local tanning salon. Her fingernails were perfect ovals, lacquered with enough plum-colored polish to make them appear wet. She wore a ring on every other finger, most of them exquisite works of art that displayed discreet—but undeniably expensive—gemstones.

For some reason he recalled Sylvie Venner's hands, the hands that had traced erratic, erotic patterns on his body that bore no resemblance to the orderly array of lines on the blueprints. Sylvie's hands were rough, red and dry—a result, no doubt, of her work behind the bar—her nails were bitten down to the quick and the only piece of jewelry she wore was her high school ring. So why was he thinking he'd rather have one of those hands next to his right now than the example of feminine perfection that lay beside him at the moment?

He banished the thought. He'd expressly forbidden himself to think about Sylvie, about that single afternoon the two of them had shared just over two weeks ago. But he couldn't help wondering if she knew by now whether their efforts of that afternoon had come to fruition. He couldn't help but wonder if she was carrying his child.

No, not *his* child, he corrected himself immediately. Sylvie had made it more than clear that he would bear no responsibility for any progeny that resulted from their union. Whatever progeny she bore would be hers and hers alone. She even had it in writing. Damn her.

"Chase?" Gwen asked beside him.

"Hmm?"

"I asked you if there was any way we could move the mezzanine elevators to the east and west wings instead of the north and south. That would put them closer to the anchor stores. Weren't you listening?"

He sighed heavily and tried to curb the impatience that sprang up out of nowhere. "I'm sorry," he told her. "I wasn't paying attention.'' He scanned the blueprints absently. ''There may be a way we can rearrange things, but it's going to require some significant structural changes. And remember that the anchor stores will have their own elevators. Can I get back to you on it?''

She smiled at him, a dazzling display of delight. ''Of course. Maybe we could talk about it over lunch. Do you have any plans?''

Not a one, he thought. Absolutely nothing to keep him from whiling away an hour with Ms. Gwendolyn Montgomery over a professional meal that might possibly become a little more social than usual, seeing as how she made no secret of her desire to get to know him better. Nothing except for the fact that he didn't want to spend any more time with her than he had to. He didn't know why. She was attractive, intelligent, had a wry sense of humor and a tremendous amount in common with him. But she wasn't . . .

He sighed once more. ''I'm sorry, Gwen,'' he apologized again. ''I have a prior engagement.''

She lifted one shoulder and dropped it in a careless shrug. ''Oh, well. Can't blame a girl for trying. Maybe some other time.''

''Maybe.''

She opened her mouth to say something else, but the intercom on his desk buzzed loudly and prevented her from doing so.

''Yes?'' Chase said as he pressed his finger to the button.

Lucille's crisp, efficient voice rattled over the line. ''A Ms. Sylvie Venner, who does not have an appointment—again— is here to see you.''

Chase smiled. If there was one thing that upended Lucille's world more than anything else, it was someone who did not abide by the rigid rules of appointment setting. He wondered what on earth Sylvie was doing there and was about to tell Lucille that he would be right out when his office door burst open. What he saw on the other side made his smile broaden. A very nice pair of legs encased in red tights and black suede boots extended beneath the hem of a black, crushed-velvet minidress. Other than that, all he could see was a huge bouquet of flowers and what appeared to be dozens of multicolored balloons.

"It's all right, Lucille," Chase said into the intercom, envisioning his by-the-book secretary leaping over her desk to halt Sylvie's interruption. "I'll take care of it."

The balloons parted some to reveal Sylvie's face, whose expression, upon her notation of Gwen's presence in the room, changed at once from radiant happiness to crestfallen disappointment.

"Oh, am I interrupting something?" she asked. "Is this a bad time?"

Chase looked over at Gwen and smiled sheepishly. "Sylvie," he said, "this is Gwendolyn Montgomery, a client of mine. Gwen, this is Sylvie Venner, my, uh...my bartender."

Gwen's eyebrows shot up at the introduction at the same time Sylvie's, Chase noted, arrowed down.

"Nice to meet you," Gwen said.

"Actually," Sylvie told her, pushing aside a purple balloon that swept in front of her face, "we've already met. Sort of. I was here a couple of weeks ago when you were in the conference room."

"Oh, yes, of course. I remember."

Sylvie smiled, seemingly pleased by the revelation.

Gwen turned to Chase, tapping an impatient index finger against the blueprints. "You know, there really are a number of other things we still need to talk about on this," she told him pointedly.

He nodded and turned to Sylvie. "I'm kind of in the middle of something here, Sylvie. How about if we discuss whatever it is you came to see me about later at Cosmo's?"

Sylvie's expression drooped again, and she began to edge her way anxiously against the far wall toward a teakwood credenza. There, as gingerly as she would a fine crystal vase, she deposited her burden of flowers and balloons. "That's okay," she said softly. "I just, um, I just wanted to stop by and say thank you." She brushed her hands off negligently on the front of her dress and tucked a strand of pale blond hair behind her ear. "It, ah, it worked," she announced with a smile that was clearly forced, her eyes wandering over everything in the room except Chase and Gwen. A spot of bright pink appeared on each cheek.

A spark of something warm and wary sputtered to life deep in Chase's midsection. He was almost afraid to ask, but he did, anyway. "What worked?"

Sylvie's gaze skittered from his to Gwen's and back to his again. She began to slowly edge her way back toward the door. "*It* did," she said. "You know. That little favor you did for me a couple of weeks ago. It worked. Everything...everything happened that was supposed to happen. And I just stopped by because I wanted to say thank you."

Chase was afraid to believe it was true, was overwhelmed by all the implications of what she was telling him. "Then that means you're..." This time it was his gaze that ricocheted from one woman to the other. "You're definitely..."

"Uh-huh," Sylvie said softly. "I am. Definitely."

Chase took a tentative step forward and stopped. "Sylvie—"

"And I just wanted to say thank you," she interrupted him. "So...thanks, Chase."

Without awaiting any further comment from him, she hastened through the door, tugging it closed swiftly behind her, a gesture that sent the multicolored balloons flying into wild motion again. Chase turned to watch them, seeing instead the way Sylvie had looked at him when she had told him she was pregnant. She'd looked pleased, he marveled. She'd looked proud. And she'd looked...dammit, she'd looked hurt, too.

And somehow he knew her distress had nothing to do with her delicate condition. But it had everything to do with the fact that he'd asked her to leave him alone with Gwen before she'd been able to tell him.

"My, what an interesting person," Gwen said dryly when the moment began to stretch into an uncomfortable silence.

Chase nodded. "That she is."

"I don't suppose I should ask what all that was about."

"No, I don't suppose you should."

He'd never felt more torn in his life. His heart commanded that he follow Sylvie immediately and press her for more details. But every rational cell in his brain told him to let her go and leave her alone. He had very important business to attend to, after all, and nothing was more crucial than keeping his current project on track. And that meant spending the rest of the afternoon with Gwen, going over a number of considerations they had yet to settle, then spending much of the evening on site double-checking the plans that would soon be fully under way.

He didn't have time for Sylvie Venner, he told himself. Since leaving Cosmo's for the last time two weeks ago, he had given himself a stern talking-to. He'd reminded himself of all the things that are really important in life—work, work and work. Nothing else. Maybe he'd allowed himself to become sidetracked for a little while, had been dazzled and flattered by Sylvie's request that he make love to her to give her a child. Maybe he'd let her infant nephew tug at a few idle heartstrings he hadn't been aware he possessed. And maybe he'd entertained a few fantasies about what it would be like to have a son of his own.

He'd granted himself a small vacation from reality, he told himself now. He'd made love to a beautiful woman—his palms still sweated when he recalled that afternoon—and he'd traveled to a little fantasy land far removed from the world in which he normally dwelt. A fantasyland that had allowed him a glimpse of how things might be different for him. How things might be if he was married with children.

And in the end he'd realized that his dreams were only that—dreams. Gwen had made him an offer he couldn't refuse, one that would command every scrap of concentration and commitment he possessed. He was a businessman, he'd reminded himself, not a family man. He didn't have the time or energy to devote to anything other than his company. That's where he found satisfaction, and that's where he found his identity. He wouldn't give up his way of life for anything. Or anyone.

Sylvie Venner was a nice kid. In turn, he was certain she would *produce* a nice kid. But he had no place in either Sylvie's life or the life of her baby. It wouldn't be fair to them.

She and her child deserved a husband and father who would give them 100 percent, who would be there when they needed him, and put them before everything else in his life. And Chase Buchanan simply wasn't that man.

So he turned to Gwen and smiled, the expression feeling false and uncomfortable as he made it. "We do still have a lot to cover," he told her. "Maybe I could cancel my engagement. Lunch sounds like a very good idea."

Seven

"Boy, you're getting big."

Sylvie stood barefoot in her underwear on the bathroom scale, sucking on a banana Popsicle and furrowing her brow at her sister's comment. Olivia and Zoey looked over each of her shoulders, shaking their heads in amazement at the number that settled beneath the needle on the dial.

"I can't believe how much weight you've gained already," Zoey said. "How far along did you say you are?"

"Sixteen weeks."

Zoey shook her head again. "Are you sure?"

"Of course I'm sure. I've been keeping a very close eye on this pregnancy."

Zoey plucked the Popsicle out of Sylvie's mouth. "Well, you better slow down on this kind of stuff. You're gaining way too fast."

"It's because of the morning sickness," Sylvie told them as she stepped off the scale. "The only thing that would settle my stomach was bacon double cheeseburgers and Snickers bars."

"Funny kind of morning sickness," Zoey mumbled, not quite under her breath.

"Oh, I don't know," Olivia told her. "When I had morning sickness, about the only thing I could keep down was potato salad. That and chocolate milk shakes."

"Well, gee, at least you were getting your calcium," Zoey muttered dryly.

"Hey, do banana Popsicles meet the same nutritional needs that real bananas do?" Sylvie asked, snatching the pale yellow confection back.

Olivia and Zoey exchanged dubious looks.

"Didn't you read that book on nutrition that I gave you?" Olivia asked.

Sylvie shook her head. "Every time I started reading about food, I threw up. It's only been in the last few weeks that the nausea has started to go away. And I'm always so exhausted when I get home from work, it's all I can do to get the newspaper read. I haven't had the energy to do much of anything else."

"Well, read that book," her sister commanded. "It's important stuff." She took the Popsicle from her sister's hand as she added, "And go eat a real banana for a change."

"And drink a big glass of milk," Zoey added.

Sylvie frowned at them and reached for her sweatpants and T-shirt, two of the few items left in her wardrobe that still fit comfortably. "Tyrants," she grumbled as the two women departed her bathroom.

Her sister and friend had been stunned by the news of her pregnancy when Sylvie had told them about it three months ago, immediately after hearing the verification from her doctor. They had been amazed that she'd actually carried out her plan, and with such immediate success.

Olivia had been especially concerned, overcome by memories of the difficulties she'd suffered going through the childbirth process alone. But Sylvie had assured her not to worry, that her situation differed completely from her sister's. For one thing, Sylvie had pointed out, she herself had set out to become pregnant intentionally, and hadn't found herself in the family way by accident, as Livy had. And when Olivia had pressed her for other differences in their situations, Sylvie had changed the subject.

She wasn't going through her pregnancy alone, she told herself again. Olivia and Zoey had both been playing an active part, just as Sylvie and Zoey had been the primary support system when Olivia was pregnant. She had her friends, Sylvie reminded herself. And they were all she would need.

But she still couldn't quite shake her memories of Chase.

She hadn't tried to contact him since that day she'd gone to his office to tell him the news and found him caught up in rapt conversation with his new *client*. And he, she reminded herself morosely, hadn't tried to contact her. She remembered the way he'd fairly chased her out of his office that day, the way he'd introduced her to the other woman as nothing more than his bartender.

She supposed she had no one but herself to blame for that. She had pretty much been responsible for fairly chasing *him* out of Cosmo's the last time he'd been there to see her. But she had thought he might take *some* interest in how she was doing.

He was probably pretty busy, too, these days, she told herself. He had a very important client now, after all.

She tied a bow in the drawstrings at her waist and went to join her companions in the living room. Simon sat in the center of the room on his brightly colored quilt, looking, Sylvie noted, nothing at all as he had the day he'd arrived in the world more than a year ago.

She wondered what her child would look like at fourteen months. She could still scarcely believe there was another human being growing to life inside her. Although she'd gained a significant amount of weight and had been forced to buy a larger size in trousers to wear to work, her belly was only slightly protruding. To the casual observer, she didn't appear to be pregnant at all. But Sylvie saw changes in her body everywhere she looked.

"You're never going to tell us who the father of this baby is, are you?" Olivia asked as she pulled her son into her lap and struggled to replace a shoe he'd managed to remove.

"It isn't important who the father is," Sylvie told her.

Olivia looked over at Zoey for support, but the other woman simply lifted her hands and offered no comment.

"It isn't," Sylvie insisted. "He's a nice guy who comes from what is obviously a fantastic gene pool. That's all that matters."

Olivia frowned at her. "Oh, he must be some prime DNA specimen if he's the kind of guy who gets a woman knocked up and then turns his back on her."

Sylvie lifted her chin defensively. "I made him promise not to meddle," she reminded her sister. "He signed a contract."

"So has he tried at all to get in touch with you since you told him about being pregnant?" Zoey asked. "You have told him about being pregnant, haven't you? He does deserve to know that much, at least, don't you think?"

Sylvie nodded. "I told him. But no, he hasn't exactly tried to get in touch with me. Like I said, I made him promise not to. And I think I sort of insulted him the last time I saw him. I didn't mean to, but..."

"Nevertheless—" Olivia began.

"Livy, please," Sylvie interrupted her. "I don't want to talk about it, okay?"

She could see that her sister was unwilling to relent, but Olivia acceded to the request, anyway. "Just promise me you'll call me whenever you need anything," she said.

"Or me," Zoey added.

"I will," Sylvie assured them. Who else was she going to call?

"I still think you should tell us who the father is," Olivia told her.

"I wouldn't mind knowing that myself," Zoey agreed.

"Why?" Sylvie demanded. "So you can hire a couple of guys from South Philly named Bruno and Sal to go over to his place and break his legs? No way."

"No," Olivia said. "So we could go have a little chat with him ourselves and make him see reason."

Sylvie stared at them. "What are you, nuts? You guys would do more damage than Bruno and Sal would."

"Sylvie..." Olivia cautioned.

"He's a very busy guy," Sylvie explained hastily. "He doesn't want a woman—or a baby—messing up his life any more than I want a man messing up mine. He's great genetic material, but his potential as a father—or husband—is nil.''

Olivia opened her mouth to object, but Sylvie halted her with a wave of her hand. "Trust me, Livy. I know men. I work around them all the time, and they tell me their most intimate secrets. Chase—'' she bit her lip when she realized she'd mentioned his name, but hurried on, hoping the other women didn't notice her gaffe ''—is ruthlessly goal oriented, very ambitious and utterly focused on his career. His work is his life. It's the only family he wants or needs.''

"Then why did he take time out of his busy, goal-oriented life to give you a baby?'' Zoey asked.

It was a question Sylvie had asked herself more than a few times since that afternoon they'd shared together what seemed like a lifetime ago. And for the life of her, she still didn't have an answer.

"I don't know,'' she told them honestly. "I just don't know.''

"Maybe you don't have this guy pegged quite so neatly as you think you do,'' Zoey told her. "Or maybe . . . maybe he doesn't know himself as well as he thinks he does.''

Sylvie looked at Zoey thoughtfully, wondering what was going on in that wily, red head of hers. As good a friend as she was, there was a lot about Zoey that neither Sylvie nor Olivia knew. She'd never opened up to the two sisters about her experiences prior to meeting Olivia in nursing school. But Sylvie sensed a well of wisdom in Zoey that resulted from whatever those experiences might have been. It was almost eerie sometimes, the insight Zoey seemed to have into human nature. And almost always, she was right on the mark when it came to identifying what made people tick.

"I think he's more sure of himself than any human being has a right to be,'' Sylvie said of Chase. "And I think he's more than certain that a wife and child don't fit into his future in any way, shape or form.''

"Which, of course, is just fine with you, right?'' Zoey asked, her voice carrying just the slightest edge of skepticism. "Seeing as how you don't want anything to do with any man.''

For some reason Sylvie suddenly felt defensive. "Of course it's fine with me," she said. "I don't have any room in my future for him, either."

"Whatever you say, Sylvie," Zoey muttered. "Whatever you say."

In his sleekly designed and elegantly decorated fifteenth-floor downtown Philadelphia condominium, Chase was dreaming. Dreaming about a blonde. A blonde with blue eyes and long, dark lashes, whose hands were soft, pink, delicate and oh so tentative against his own. And her smile...he almost sighed in his sleep. Her smile was like none he'd ever seen before. Because it was wide and gorgeous and displayed a total of four perfect teeth.

His eyes snapped open, and he gasped in a ragged breath. A baby. God, he'd been dreaming about a baby. A baby girl who was an absolute miniature of a woman he hadn't seen for more than four months. Obviously Sylvie Venner hadn't been far from his thoughts in all that time, however. Now she was even invading his dreams. At least, childish versions of her were invading his dreams. He couldn't imagine what had caused such a nighttime fantasy.

He squinted at the clock on the nightstand, the glowing green numerals informing him that it wasn't yet three-thirty, so he still had a good two hours of sleeping to do before he was forced to rise. He punched his pillow fretfully, recalled once again the ghostly baby that had floated up from nowhere in his brain, turned onto his other side and closed his eyes. But before he'd taken another breath, the phone rang shrilly mere inches from his head, and he bolted up in bed.

Who on earth would have the temerity to telephone him at this hour? he wondered before deciding it was probably a wrong number. Some drunken sot had no doubt been out trying to drown his sorrows over a woman and thought he had punched the numbers of his beloved's abode instead.

Chase lay back down and closed his eyes, deciding to let the answering machine earn its keep. He heard his own solid, to-the-point message, then a quick beep, and then a woman's voice.

"Chase? Chase, are you home? If you're there, please, *please* answer the phone. I need you."

He recognized the voice immediately and jackknifed up in bed, leaping for the machine to punch the Off button at the same time he jerked up the phone. "Sylvie?" he rasped out, his own voice still rough from sleep. "What is it? What's wrong?"

She hesitated for only a moment, then continued in a hurried, frightened tone, "Can you come over? I need you. Right away. It's an emergency."

He ran a big hand through his sleep-rumpled hair, more than a little concerned by her unmistakable fear. "Are you all right?" he demanded. Then he remembered she was pregnant. The baby. Oh, God, the baby. "Is it..." He inhaled deeply, hoping to steady himself. "The baby, Sylvie. Is everything okay with the baby?"

"I don't know. I feel...I'm so... Oh, Chase, can you please come over?"

"Where are you, at home?"

"Yes." Her voice broke on a strangled sob, and she started to cry.

Reeling with the frustration and helplessness the soft, muffled sounds roused in him, he wished desperately that he could reach into the telephone receiver to touch her. Instead, he growled, "I'll be there as soon as I can."

He didn't wait to hear her say goodbye, didn't waste any more breath of his own. He simply dropped the receiver back into its cradle, reached for the nearest clothes he could find—in this case a pair of exhausted, baggy khakis and a loose-fitting, faded red T-shirt—shoved his feet into his shoes without socks and ran for the front door.

Sylvie, he thought. God, Sylvie. The last time he had seen her, she had been thanking him for giving her a child. Since then he'd returned to Cosmo's on his usual schedule only to be told that Sylvie Venner had switched over to the day shift. He'd taken that as an unequivocal sign that she never wanted to see him again. He'd fulfilled his obligation to her and, true to her contractual assertions, she wanted nothing more from him.

So he'd thrown himself full force into his new project for Montgomery Construction, Inc., focusing 100 percent of his concentration on that in an effort to dispel any lingering images of the afternoon he and Sylvie had spent together so many months ago. Nevertheless, memories of that time—and of Sylvie—continued to invade his brain at the most inopportune moments, usually when his guard was down and he was least expecting them.

And on those occasions, when he remembered her funky clothes and bright smile, the ease with which the two of them had always communicated and her affinity for making him laugh, Chase always wished things had turned out differently between them.

He shouldn't have gone so long without contacting her, he thought as he grabbed his car keys and raced for his front door. He should have made sure months ago that she was all right, that everything with the baby was moving along as it should be. Even if she'd reacted to his concern by pushing him away and reminding him that her life was none of his business, at least he would have been able to reassure himself that she was okay. At least he would have let her know that no matter what, he still cared about her.

He ran to the end of the corridor and punched the elevator button, then paced restlessly back and forth as he watched the numbers above the doors light up slowly as the car ascended. "Come on, dammit," he muttered under his breath, not sure whether he was talking to the elevator, to Sylvie or to himself. "Come on."

Sylvie's eyes were wet and red rimmed when she opened her front door twenty minutes later. Somehow Chase noted that she was dressed only in an oversize T-shirt advertising the restaurant where she worked, but before he could say a word to her, she threw herself against him, wrapping her arms around his neck, holding on to him with all her might.

Vaguely he registered the feel of her slightly rounded belly against his lower abdomen, then he lost himself in the scent of her hair, a fresh, powdery fragrance that at once reminded him of how unbelievably satisfying it had been to make love to her. He draped one arm around her shoulders and circled one around her waist, and she slumped against him in gratitude as if she alone were no longer able to keep herself standing.

"What is it?" he asked quietly as he kicked the front door closed behind himself. "Are you hurt? Is there something wrong with the baby?"

Sylvie started to cry again, sobbing softly against his chest as she curled her fingers into the fabric of his T-shirt.

"Sylvie?" he said, feeling a cold void open in the pit of his stomach. Now he began to grow frightened, too. "Is everything okay? What is it? What's wrong?"

She mumbled something against his shirt, garbled words he couldn't possibly understand.

"What?" he asked.

She pushed herself away only far enough to look at him, and studied his face intently. The presence of tears made her eyes seem huge and bluer than ever. She sniffled once, blinked and palmed at a single runaway tear. "I...I had a bad dream," she finally told him.

Chase stared at her incredulously, certain he must have misunderstood. "A bad dream," he repeated evenly. "You woke me up in the middle of the night, brought me out of my safe condo to run over here at a time when there's no one but thugs out on the streets, scared the absolute hell out of me...." He took a deep breath to steady his nerves. "You did all that because you had a bad dream?"

Sylvie sniffled again and nodded. "It was a really bad dream."

He should be angry with her, he thought. He should tell her she was being ridiculous, order her back to bed, then go home and try to salvage what he could of the night to get some much-needed rest. Instead, he folded his arms around her again, settled his chin on the top of her head and sighed.

"Do you want to talk about it?" he asked.

He felt her nod as she whispered, "Yes."

He held her for a moment longer, squeezed her gently, then led her over to her couch. But instead of joining her there, he went to her kitchen and opened the cabinet where he recalled she kept her dishes, took out a glass, and then went to the refrigerator. After filling the glass with milk, he returned to the living room, extending the drink toward her. Sylvie only looked at it for a moment, then glanced up to meet his gaze.

"Would you like me to warm it up for you?" he asked.

She smiled. Not a very big smile, he noted, but it was certainly more reassuring than the sniffling and tears he'd witnessed only moments earlier. "No, that's okay," she said as her fingers closed around the glass. "Thanks."

He sat beside her, watching as she sipped her milk and stared at his feet.

"I've never seen you dressed like this before," she finally said, still gazing down at the floor. "So... so casual and relaxed. You're not even wearing any socks."

His gaze followed hers. "Neither are you."

"That's because I was sleeping."

He waited until she was looking at his face again before replying, "So was I."

She smiled a little anxiously and sipped her milk again. Chase remained silent as she completed the action, trying his best to hang on to a stern expression in spite of the warm, squishy things that seeing her this way made him feel inside. It was good to be with Sylvie again, he thought. He didn't care what time it was.

"I'm sorry," she said as she set the glass down on her coffee table. She continued to avoid looking at him as she went on, "I just... I had this horrible, horrible dream and I woke up terrified. I didn't know what else to do, didn't know who else to call. After I hung up from you, I remembered that I could have called Livy and Daniel, or Zoey. But they all live in New Jersey, and it would have taken them forever to get here, and you..." She shrugged apologetically and finally glanced up to meet his gaze. "You were the first person I thought about after... after—"

"It's all right, Sylvie," he told her, flattered and heartened by the fact that she'd thought of him before she'd even considered the members of her own family or her closest friend. Almost without thinking about it, he lifted his hand to her shoulder and skimmed his fingers lightly over her back. "Do you want to tell me about it?"

Sylvie inhaled deeply and released her breath slowly, then nodded. She could scarcely believe Chase was there with her. She had spent months trying to forget about him, trying to rid herself of the memory of that single afternoon they'd spent together. And until a little while ago she'd been convinced that she had effectively put him out of her thoughts, out of her life forever.

But when she'd awakened from her nightmare, horrified by the dream that had risen so vividly in her brain while she slept, all she'd been able to think about was Chase and how much she needed him there with her. She hadn't even thought about what she was doing when she reached for the phone book to search for his number, couldn't now remember what she had even said when she'd spoken to him on the phone. She only knew that he had rushed right over to be with her, in spite of the ungodly hour. He hadn't even taken the time to put on his socks.

"In the dream," she began slowly, unwilling to relive the terror but helpless not to talk about it, "I was in the hospital. I'd just had the baby. At first everything was so peaceful and wonderful. I just held the baby in my arms and stared at her, and she stared back at me. It was a girl," she added unnecessarily. "I had a girl. She was fat and pink and perfect and . . . and beautiful."

When Sylvie looked at Chase there was a strange kind of fire kindling to life in his eyes, but she couldn't even begin to imagine what he was thinking. The fingers drawing leisurely circles on her back stilled, and an odd serenity seemed to settle over the living room. Outside the night was silent, and she somehow began to feel as if she and Chase were the only living souls in the universe.

"I sang to her, even called her Genevieve," she went on softly, her eyes never leaving his, "which is what I've kind of decided to name the baby if it's a girl."

"I like it," he said softly, his hand beginning the idle caress on her back again. "I had a grandmother named Genevieve."

She smiled. "Really?"

He nodded. "So what happened to turn such a lovely vision into such a terrible nightmare?"

Sylvie wished she could forget about that part. "Well, I was holding her in my arms, and suddenly she went limp. She just...went limp. A nurse came running over and snatched her away from me saying that I'd done something wrong, that the baby was dying. I jumped out of bed and followed her down the hall to another room that was filled with doctors and more nurses and all kinds of medical equipment. Everyone was racing around, and they hooked Genevieve up to some machine, but something went wrong."

Sylvie felt her eyes filling with tears at the memory, and she swiped them away, only to have them reappear. "The next thing I knew they were telling me...they were telling me she was dead."

"Oh, Sylvie."

"And they wouldn't let me see her," she went on, her tears coming in earnest again. She leaned toward him, and he folded his arms around her. "It all happened so fast," she mumbled against him. "One minute everything was peaceful and wonderful, and the next minute...the next minute..."

"Shh," he said, stroking his hand over her hair, pulling her close again.

"They wouldn't let me see her," Sylvie went on relentlessly. "They just kept telling me she was dead. And I started shouting out, 'No, no, no.' And when I woke up I was still shouting out, 'No, no, no....'"

"Shh," he repeated, holding her more tightly. "Don't think about it. It was only a dream. A bad dream, granted, but just a dream. It's okay, Sylvie. You're okay. And I'm sure the baby is fine, too."

He rocked her as if she were a child, and all Sylvie could do was let him. It felt good to have him there, and any misgivings she'd had about calling him in the first place evaporated. She closed her eyes and let him comfort her, thinking how wonderful it felt not to be alone. Instinctively she curled her hand over her womb, hoping she might feel evidence of the life growing inside her, wishing for one little flutter that might reassure her that the baby was just fine.

But she felt nothing. It was still too early, she told herself. The baby was still too small. The reminders were little comfort, however. And she couldn't quite shake the anxiety that still wound through her.

She felt Chase's hand cover hers then, his big fingers dwarfing hers, his palm warm against the back of her hand. "What is it?" he asked her.

She sighed heavily, still leaning against him. "Nothing. It's too early for me to feel anything. I was just hoping maybe the baby would give me some kind of sign."

"He will," Chase said, his voice exuding confidence. "In time, he'll be kicking up a storm."

Sylvie smiled and pulled away enough to look up at his face. "He?" she asked. "Are you so sure it's going to be a boy?"

"Are you so sure it's going to be a girl?" he countered.

"According to my dream, it is."

He shook his head. "That was just a dream. That bun you have in the oven is of the masculine persuasion. I know it."

"Oh, and just how do you know?"

Chase puffed up his chest proudly. "A man can tell these things about his own child."

His insistence that the baby was his own put Sylvie's back up defensively. Their two hands were still cupped over the curve of her belly, and she tugged hers out from beneath his. Chase, however, kept his hand where it was, pressing his fingers more tightly against her.

"This isn't your baby, Chase," she said softly. "It's mine."

He dropped his gaze to her abdomen, slowly rubbing his hand across the soft mound to the other side. Sylvie sucked in a silent breath and held it. Clearly he was completely unaware of how it felt to have him touching her so intimately. However, she couldn't help but take notice.

"Maybe," he said softly. "But you did have a little help creating it."

This time it was Sylvie who covered Chase's hand with hers, lifting it cautiously away from her belly. "Help that has come and gone from my life," she said quietly. "From here on out, I'm on my own. It's just me and my baby."

He looked at her as she dropped their hands to the sofa cushion between their bodies. Sylvie was suddenly all too aware of how little she was wearing, but instead of feeling cold, she became inexplicably, and almost unbearably, warm. Chase's expression changed immediately, and she knew he had begun to understand what his simple touch had done to her. He lifted his free hand to her face, cupping her jaw softly before raking the backs of his fingers across her cheek and tangling them in her hair.

"I've missed you," he said, the words seeming drawn from him reluctantly. "Every time I go into Cosmo's I still expect to see you there, and when you're not, it wrecks my day. I haven't stopped thinking about you. I haven't been able to forget about that one afternoon. I've been wondering how you were doing, how you were feeling. Wondering if you needed anything." He dropped his gaze to their entwined hands. "I shouldn't have let so much time pass without checking up on you."

Sylvie tried to feel offended by the proprietary nature of his statement, tried to remind herself that assertions like his were exactly why she didn't want a man meddling in her life. She could take care of herself just fine, thanks, and had been for years. She knew she should tell Chase that, knew she should make it perfectly clear. But something about the way he made his statement halted any objection she might utter.

"I'm fine," she told him. "Until tonight I've been fine pretty much all along. I had morning sickness for the first few months, but that's gone now."

"You were sick?" The obvious concern in his voice tugged at something deep down inside her she hadn't felt for a very long time. "You should have called me."

"It's okay. There was nothing you could have done."

"I could have come over and taken care of you. Made sure you were comfortable."

She knew he was speaking the truth, knew that if she had called him during those early months of nausea, he would have come over and plied her with chicken noodle soup and club soda. The realization made her feel at once comforted and threatened. Comforted because it would have been nice to have someone there babying her when she felt lousy. And threatened because she didn't want anyone insinuating himself into her life to such a large—such a familiar—degree.

The conflicting emotions confused Sylvie, and she reacted as she usually did when faced with such a dilemma. She retreated. Jumping up from the sofa, she snatched her glass of milk from the coffee table, downed what was left with one big gulp and hurried off to the kitchen.

"Thanks for coming over," she said as she rinsed out the glass and refilled it with cold water from the tap. She sipped thirstily, but the icy liquid did little to cool the heat that was winding quickly through her body. She turned abruptly to face Chase again. "But I think I'll be okay now," she told him shakily. "There's no reason for you to lose any more sleep over me."

Chase stood and sauntered toward her, pausing to lean his forearms on the breakfast bar that separated the kitchen from the living room. He seemed to be thinking hard about something, seemed ready to make a speech, and Sylvie was afraid to hear whatever it was he might have to say.

Finally he uttered quietly, "Something tells me I'll be losing a lot of sleep over you from here on out."

Something in his voice made her heart skip a beat, made a hot flush shimmy up her body from her toes to her face. "Why?" she asked, the single word scarcely audible in the silent room.

He didn't answer her right away. Instead he only stared at her as if he were seeing her for the first time. A muscle twitched in his jaw, and his gaze was steely intense. Finally he pushed himself away from the breakfast bar and dropped his hands to his hips.

"You're sure you'll be all right tonight?" he asked her.

For some reason Sylvie was surprised by how easily he had acquiesced to her request that he leave and go back home. She had thought he would argue, had expected that he would insist on spending the night to make sure no more nightmarish bugaboos ruined her sleep. Instead, he seemed fully ready and anxious to make his escape.

Which, of course, was fine with her, she told herself. She never should have telephoned him in the first place. She couldn't imagine what she had been thinking when she did.

"Yes," she finally said. "I'm sure."

He nodded, then turned and headed for the front door. She thought he was going to leave without another word or a backward glance, but just as he settled his hand over the knob, he paused.

"Will you call me if you...if something like this happens again?" he asked quietly without looking at her.

Sylvie wasn't sure if he wanted her to reply yes or no. So she simply responded in the only way she knew how. She told him the truth. "No, I won't. I'm sorry I even called you tonight. It was a mistake. I promise not to bother you again. You're off the hook."

She thought he intended to say something more, but he just shook his head almost imperceptibly. "I'll be in touch," he said simply before tugging the door open and passing through it.

And before Sylvie could utter a single word in protest, Chase was gone.

Eight

It was the shoes, Chase decided, that primarily captured his attention and held it. Black high top sneakers, really nothing out of the ordinary. He'd had a pair almost exactly like them when he was in high school. But these shoes differed from the ones he had owned in one minor respect. These particular black high tops were only about four inches long. And instead of being worn by a lanky teenager intent on a serious game of basketball, the shoes were attached to a chubby little baby who couldn't possibly be old enough to walk.

As Chase sat alone at a corner table in a downtown deli waiting for his lunch, he tried his damnedest to concentrate on the business section of the *Inquirer*. Instead, his gaze kept wandering back to the table next to his, where two young women chatted as old friends do, one of them feeding lunch to her small child. The baby sucked eagerly at the bottle she held in her hand, but his gaze was fixed steadily on Chase. In addition to the tiny black high tops, he wore denim overalls and a red striped T-shirt, a red baseball cap perched backward atop his bald little head. Chase had never seen such a chicly attired baby before. He wondered if this was some new trend, this dressing of babies as if they were a part of the MTV generation.

When the waitress set a cup of coffee on the table before him, Chase returned his attention to the newspaper he had nearly forgotten and went back to his reading. But a cry from the baby brought his notice around again. The baby's mother had lifted him to her shoulder and was patting his back gently, in an effort, Chase assumed, to burp the little guy. That's what people did after they fed babies, wasn't it? he thought. That's the way it worked on television and in movies. At least, that's how he thought it worked. He'd never really known any babies—or mothers, for that matter. Not until he'd met Sylvie Venner and her nephew.

For the second time in less than five months Chase was finding himself fascinated by the workings of a baby. What a strange development for someone who had never before considered such beings noteworthy in any way. He sipped his coffee and began to read the paper again, but his gaze was inexplicably drawn back to the little boy. He watched as the mother continued to pat the child's back softly, taking in every aspect of her posture and her movements. Finally the baby released a little hiccup and smiled. It was the same four-toothed smile Chase had received from Sylvie's nephew, and that same odd thrill of enjoyment rippled through him as a result.

This wasn't normal, Chase thought. It couldn't possibly be. What he felt inside simply wasn't the kind of reaction grown men had because they just so happened upon a cute little kid. Not grown men like him, anyway. Not grown men who had more important things on their minds. Things like building a business and keeping it thriving. Things like multimillion dollar projects that commanded every bit of their mental stamina.

The two women finished their lunch and paid their bill, and the boy's mother tucked him into a stroller and collected her things. Chase watched as the trio departed, the baby peeking out of the stroller behind himself at Chase as they left. All the way out of the deli the baby watched him, until mother and child were completely out of sight. For a long moment Chase only stared at the door through which the baby had passed, seeing not the infant's brown eyes staring back at him from beneath a red baseball cap, but green eyes instead. Green eyes like his own.

When he realized the avenue down which his thoughts were so errantly wandering, Chase sighed in exasperation. Rattling the newspaper in his hands to straighten it, he began to read for the fourth time an article about his own new fashion mall whose construction was thoroughly under way. But by the time he had come to the end of the story he'd completely forgotten everything he'd read.

An entire weekend off, Sylvie marveled the Friday night after Chase had come to rescue her from her bad dream. She hummed happily under her breath as she scraped the last remnants of her dinner from the plate and rinsed it off. Such a precious commodity was a weekend off, such a rare occurrence. Two full days she could gloriously call her own, two full days with which she could do whatever she pleased. She could go anywhere, do anything, be whatever she wanted to be.

She sighed deeply. Two full days off from work, and here she was, all by herself. Livy and Daniel had packed up Simon and run off to Cape May for the weekend, and Zoey was in Pittsburgh, visiting her two aunts. The rest of Sylvie's friends all seemed to be working, so where did that leave her? On her own, she thought dejectedly. All alone.

Almost without thinking about it, she spread her hand open over the small mound that bulged beneath her loose, flowered cotton jumper. No, not entirely alone, she thought with a little smile.

She took her cup of decaffeinated coffee and went to the living room to enjoy it, staring through the French doors that led to her terrace out at the midsummer sky beyond. It was hazy and tinted brown as it always seemed to be during the summer months, and she thought about how nice it would be to get away for the weekend, too. But the Jersey shore was as bad as the city, she reminded herself, crowded with hordes of tourists and weekenders scattering all manner of litter, not to mention the occasional unidentified flotsam and jetsam washing up on shore.

Maybe she'd move to the suburbs after the baby came, she thought suddenly. She loved living in the city, but it would be nice for her child to have a yard in which to play. Maybe Sylvie could learn how to garden, at least learn to master a window box, and grow her own vegetables and herbs. She and the baby could take long strolls around the neighborhood at dusk, and she could meet other moms who had children her child's age. Maybe, eventually, the two of them could even get a puppy.

Sylvie had settled quite nicely into her fantasy of tranquil, verdant suburban life when the vision was rudely interrupted by a knock at her front door. Her head snapped around at the intrusive sound, and as she crossed the living room to answer the door she was overcome by a feeling of foreboding. Somehow she knew who she would find standing in the hallway on the other side, and she curled her fingers over the knob with some trepidation.

"Hi," Chase said when she opened the door to him.

She noted only absently the two bulging paper grocery sacks he held in his arms, so intent was she on taking in the rest of his attire. He wore faded, thigh-hugging blue jeans, an equally faded polo shirt that had probably once been a rich forest green, and well-weathered leather sneakers. He looked considerably less like the high-powered businessman with whom she had so little in common and quite a lot like most of the guys she had dated before her rendezvous with Chase.

"Hi," she returned, wondering what on earth she could say to make him leave without sounding too horribly impolite.

"I came over to fix you dinner," he stated without preamble, making his way past her. He headed immediately toward her kitchen as if he had lived in the apartment as long as she had. "I noticed the other night that you don't seem to have too much food in your refrigerator."

Sylvie followed him and stood by helplessly as he placed his burden on the counter and turned to face her.

"I have plenty of food in my fridge," she countered.

Chase smiled and moved quickly to the appliance in question, tugging open the door with much familiarity. "A half gallon of milk, a bottle of orange juice, two cartons of yogurt, a tub of butter and three hard-boiled eggs. Oh, and a bag of bagels that don't look anywhere near fresh. That hardly constitutes 'plenty.'"

Sylvie crossed her arms over her chest defensively. "There are some apples in the crisper," she told him haughtily. "*And* a package of those little baby carrots." Or had she eaten those? she wondered now. "I think."

"You're eating for two now, Sylvie," he reminded her, returning to his groceries. "You have to think about every bite of food you put in your mouth."

"I always have a salad on my lunch break at Cosmo's," she said. "And I usually have dinner at the restaurant before I come home. I get plenty to eat."

"Oh, sure," he countered. "Spicy, rich foods covered with heavy sauces and maybe a couple of vegetables equally loaded down. That's way too much fat, and not at all conducive to good eating habits. Nutrition is extremely important during pregnancy."

She rolled her eyes heavenward. "Have you been talking to my sister?"

He turned again, looking clearly surprised. "No. I've been doing some reading."

"About nutrition?"

"About nutrition during pregnancy." He turned back to the bags as he added, almost under his breath, "Among other things."

Sylvie narrowed her eyes suspiciously. "What other things?"

He began plucking groceries out of the bags and sorting them on her counter as if the activity were something he performed on a regular basis. Most of the items, she noted, were from the section of the grocery store she normally ignored—produce. She wrinkled her nose in disgust at the fresh vegetables. Broccoli? she thought when he extracted a huge bunch. Ick.

"Have you thought about what childbirth method you're going to use when the time comes to deliver?" he asked.

Well, there was a question out of the blue, Sylvie thought. "Yeah," she told him. "I've pretty much decided I want to be completely unconscious during the delivery. It doesn't matter what they have to give me. Even a quick, solid blow to the back of the head would be fine.''

He paused in his actions to glare at her.

She nodded. ''Either that or I'm going to ask them to bring me a big bottle of Scotch, a six-pack of club soda and a half dozen lemons. After six or seven cocktails I should be pretty much ready. Heck, the whole medical team can party with me until the baby arrives.''

His glare intensified.

She expelled an exasperated breath. ''I'm kidding!'' she cried, coming to stand beside him. ''Geez, you just have no sense of humor at all.'' At his expression of utter dismay, she relented a little. ''Okay, okay. I haven't decided yet what method I'm going to use. I still don't know too much about it. I have a lot of reading left to do.''

Chase nodded. ''Well, I've been reading about this Dick Grantly-Read method, and it seems to make a lot of sense. But you have to get an early start. How far along are you now? About twenty-one weeks?''

Sylvie shook her head at him in amazement. Where was all this sudden interest coming from? ''Twenty-two,'' she said simply, though why she was bothering, she didn't know. It really wasn't any of his business.

He frowned thoughtfully. ''Hmm. That's more than halfway through. It may be too late to start that one.'' He went back to unloading groceries. ''Oh, well. There's always Lamaze.''

''Chase?'' she asked, trying to keep her voice as nonchalant as possible.

''Hmm?''

''What are you doing here?''

He went back to unloading groceries as he said, ''I told you. I'm going to fix you some dinner.''

''But I've already eaten dinner.''

''And what did you have? Lobster Newburg? Cosmo's special stuffed quail with béarnaise sauce?''

''No, I didn't eat at the restaurant tonight.''

''Oh, so you fixed your *own* dinner,'' Chase said indulgently. ''No doubt it was something *really* nutritious, then.''

Sylvie hedged, biting her lip. Actually, she had sort of planned to have dinner later. What she'd had most recently was more like dessert.

"Mmm," she began.

He turned to look at her, and she could see that he was more than a little suspicious. "Well?"

"I, uh . . ."

"Sylvie, what did you have for dinner?"

"Chocolate cake," she finally confessed.

His eyes widened in shock. "Chocolate cake?" he exclaimed, sounding as he probably would if she had told him she'd just ingested drain cleaner. "What are you, nuts? Don't you realize that's nothing but empty calories?"

He yanked a book from the bottom of the grocery sack, then thumbed quickly through the pages until he found the passage he'd been searching for. He thrust the open book toward her, pointing with his finger as he continued brusquely, "Look. Right here in *Your Good Nutrition Guide to Pregnancy,* on page seventy-two, it says, and I quote—" he brought the book back toward himself to read "—'Cakes, cookies and pies are empty calories, and are of no nutritional value to you or your baby. They should be avoided.' End quote." He stared at her, shaking his head, clearly disgusted. "Yet here you stand, telling me you ate a piece of chocolate cake for dinner."

Sylvie stared down at her hands, rubbing away a few incriminating smudges of icing as she clarified, "Um, not a piece of chocolate cake, exactly. Chocolate cake."

Chase's mouth dropped open in disbelief as understanding dawned. "You ate an entire chocolate cake? For dinner?"

"Well it's not like it was a *layer* cake, for God's sake," she said in her defense. "Just one of those little Sara Lee things that comes in a foil pan." She shrugged philosophically. "I was hungry, all right? Chocolate cake sounded really good. I was going to eat something more substantial later. Honest."

She reached for one of the grocery sacks to peek inside. "Say, did you by any chance buy some ice cream with all that stuff? A couple of scoops of chocolate chipmunk would go really well with chocolate cake. And I'm still pretty hungry."

He dropped his hands to his hips in defiance. "No, I did not buy ice cream," he told her. He indicated the assortment of items he had unpacked onto the counter. "I bought oranges, tofu, wheat germ—I don't think you've been getting enough protein—lima beans—did you know that they're loaded with iron?—broccoli and brussels sprouts—"

"Brussels sprouts?" she groaned. "Ew. Gross."

"Folic acid," he said simply, as if that explained everything.

Sylvie arched her eyebrows in question as she asked hopefully, "Twinkies?"

Chase shook his head in disgust again. "What do you think?"

She sighed. "I think I'm about to be cooked the yuckiest meal of my life."

He smiled at her acquiescence and went back to work. "You can thank me later. Now, where do you keep your steamer?"

Sylvie looked at him, confused. "What's a steamer?"

It wasn't enough that Chase had coerced her into choking down foods unlike any she'd ever been forced to eat before, Sylvie thought some time later as he squeezed his expensive sports car into a tiny parking space in Fairmont Park. Oh, no, that wasn't nearly enough. She looked out the passenger-side window at the joggers and walkers making their way along the edge of Wissahickon Creek and frowned. The only thing worse than broccoli, she thought, was exercise.

Chase threw the gearshift into Park and turned off the ignition. He, too, stared out at the array of runners and walkers, the slowly descending sun turning the silver fires in his black hair to amber. His dark aviator sunglasses hid any expression he might carry in his eyes, and she wondered how someone so handsome could be so ruthless.

"You need this, Sylvie," he told her, as if reading her thoughts. "Exercise is extremely important during pregnancy. And since it's too late for you to get started on something very intensive, walking will be the perfect work-out."

"I don't want to," she said petulantly.

To defy him, she had refused to change her clothes and still wore the flowered jumper. And instead of sneakers she had slipped on a pair of flat sandals over her white cotton anklets. Maybe he could make her eat brussels sprouts, she thought, but she'd never let him see her sweat.

"Come on," he said as he pushed his door open and got out. "You'll feel a lot better after it's over."

Chase watched as Sylvie thrust open the other door and hauled herself out of the passenger seat, trying to hide his smile when she narrowed her eyes and glared at him across the top of his car. Evidently he didn't do a very good job of masking his good humor, though, because her frown only intensified before she slammed the door with enough force to rock the little red Porsche like an upset turtle. He winced in silence.

"I get plenty of exercise at work," she said as she followed with much reluctance behind him. "I run up and down behind the bar and carry stock out from the walk-in. I do more than pump iron—I pump liquor all day long. Look at these biceps," she said, flexing her arm in demonstration.

Chase wrapped his fingers around her upper arm and squeezed hard. "Impressive."

"Damn straight," she muttered. "And that's not even my pouring arm."

He skimmed his fingers down the length of her arm, noting the goose bumps his touch seemed to leave in its wake. He smiled as he circled her wrist, then entwined his fingers with hers. "We can start off slowly," he said softly, knowing it wasn't just the walking he was talking about.

Sylvie bumped along behind him hesitantly, but didn't seem quite as averse to the notion of physical activity as she had been earlier at her apartment when he'd initially proposed this excursion. The slowly setting sun bathed her hair in orange and gave her face a rosy glow that made him smile. She'd gained weight noticeably in the past few months. Even beneath the shapeless dress she wore, he could tell that her breasts and hips were rounder than he recalled. Her face, too, seemed to have filled out, and he thought the changes in her most becoming.

"You know," he began again as they strolled along the river, "it's interesting you should mention your work just now."

Sylvie slid a pair of tortoiseshell sunglasses over her eyes and gazed at him. "Why?"

How could he go about this without sounding like a complete interloper? Chase wondered. She was already mad at him just for making her dinner and insisting she take a walk with him. How was she going to react to his next request? Might as well just speak the words and get them over with, he decided.

"Because I'm wondering if maybe what you do for a living isn't just a little too strenuous for a pregnant woman," he said quickly. "You're on your feet all day," he rushed on before she could respond, "and you do a lot of heavy lifting. It's good that you've gone to daytime hours and all so that you can get plenty of sleep, but I think it might be even better if you took a leave of absence until after the baby arrives."

Her sunglasses hid any reaction he might have detected in her eyes, but he could pretty much get the gist of her emotions by the way she immediately stopped walking. That and the way her grip tightened convulsively on his.

"Sylvie," he said, forcing a light chuckle as he tried to pry their hands apart. "Let go. You're hurting me."

Her fingers pressed even harder into his.

"Ow," he said. "Look, I'm not kidding. That hurts. You're cutting off my circulation."

Immediately she turned him loose, but she continued to stand perfectly still, just staring at him.

"Sylvie?" he asked again.

"And just what," she said, her voice a lot more controlled than he had expected it would be, "am I supposed to do for a paycheck while I'm taking this leave of absence?"

Chase drew in a cautious breath. When he had first conceived of his idea, it had seemed like a good one to him. It had been business, he'd thought then. Good business. And being a businessman, the concept had made complete sense to him. Faced with explaining the particulars to Sylvie now, however, he began to wonder if maybe he hadn't been a bit rash in thinking she'd go along so easily.

"Well," he began slowly, "I thought that if money was going to be a problem for you, then maybe I could bankroll you for that period of time myself."

Her mouth dropped open in what he could only liken to outrage, and he suddenly wondered if maybe he couldn't have gone about proposing his suggestion in a better way.

"You thought *what?*" she exclaimed.

"Now, Sylvie, think about this for a minute before you go flying off the—"

"Bankroll me?" she repeated incredulously, ignoring his attempt to explain. "I don't need bankrolling. As I mentioned before, I am very financially secure, more than capable of taking care of myself and my child."

"Sylvie, I didn't mean—"

"And there's absolutely no reason for me to quit working now. I've already told Cosmo I'm taking two months after the baby comes, and he's been a good enough guy to keep me on the payroll during that time. Granted, I'll be without tips, which is the majority of my income, but I thought it was awfully decent of him to do something like that when he wasn't legally obligated."

"But don't you think it would be better if—"

"My job isn't any more strenuous than what a lot of women—a lot of *pregnant* women—do," she continued relentlessly. "I've seen pregnant women on road crews, for pete's sake. And pioneer women gave birth while plowing the fields." She pointed to her softly rounded belly. "This isn't an incapacitating affliction," she told him. "Quite the contrary. I'm going to have a baby. I'm going to be giving birth before long. Don't you think that requires some small amount of stamina? Some small degree of strength? It's ridiculous to think I need coddling, Chase. I'm not helpless. I'll be just fine."

"But all that heavy lifting," he said, knowing he'd already lost this disagreement profoundly.

"If I think something at work is too heavy for me, I get one of the guys to lift it for me," she said. "I've always done that, even before I was pregnant. I'm not stupid, after all. And they certainly don't mind helping me out."

"But being on your feet all day." He tried again.

She shrugged. "I'm no different from thousands of other pregnant women who work. There's absolutely no reason to be concerned. And besides," she added quietly, "none of that matters, anyway."

"Why not?"

She took his hand in hers and began to walk with him again. "Because it's none of your business what I do," she said simply. Her voice carried no venom, no bitterness, no anger. Just a matter-of-fact frankness that he was forced to admit was justified.

"But I worry about you, Sylvie," he said. "I just want to make sure you're okay."

"I'm okay, Chase. So stop worrying."

He wished it was that easy. And really, he thought, there was no reason it *shouldn't* be that easy. He had made a deal with Sylvie some months ago, and there was no reason he shouldn't be able to stick to it. He had too much going on in his work—his life—right now, to have time to worry about a pregnant woman. Never mind the fact that he'd been instrumental in her being put in that condition. She'd asked him to get her pregnant, after all, and then had made him promise not to involve himself further. That had seemed like such a simple request at the time, he thought now. So why couldn't he just abide by the rules the two of them had set down?

"Okay, I'll try to stop worrying," he finally said. "But I'm not sure I can promise to stay uninvolved."

Sylvie's pace slowed only slightly, only enough to let him know that the words he'd spoken troubled her. "You've already promised to stay uninvolved," she reminded him. "You signed a contract."

A contract meant to protect him as much as it did Sylvie and her baby, he realized. The more he thought about this whole arrangement, the more confused he became. And having her warm fingers linked with his as the two of them

strolled peacefully through the park at the end of a beautiful summer day wasn't helping matters at all.

He looked over at her, letting his gaze travel from her sun-
warmed face to the soft mound of belly under her jumper.
No, Chase thought again, this wasn't helping at all.

Nine

Two weeks later Sylvie was still thinking about that odd encounter with Chase. He had remained strangely quiet and uncommunicative after her reassurances that he had no business butting into her life, and had simply walked along beside her in the park in almost total silence. The drive home had been equally restrained, with Chase simply dropping her off in front of her apartment building with a brief goodbye and a swift, albeit stirring, kiss on the cheek.

Almost involuntarily she lifted her hand to her face, tracing her fingers lightly over her jaw in exactly the spot he had touched with his lips. Even with so chaste a gesture, he had made her feel giddy inside.

At the time she had been stunned by his seemingly automatic action, and by the genuine affection from which that kiss had seemed to result. In fact, she continued to be amazed. She had gained more weight in the past five months than any woman—pregnant or otherwise—should be gaining, and the unfamiliar girth made her movements feel awkward and unwieldy already. Instead of having the healthy glow of pregnancy she had heard so much about, Sylvie's skin had erupted in outbreaks unlike any she'd seen since her adolescent years. Her hair, although thicker than it had ever been before, was unmanageable and refused to behave.

She was, to her way of thinking, unsightly. Yet with one simple kiss, Chase had made her feel beautiful, as if he had been unaffected by all of those things.

That wasn't how men were supposed to act, she thought now. They were supposed to be first and foremost moved by the way a woman looked, by the superficial manner in which she presented herself physically. They responded only to outward beauty. Yet Chase had seen past all the changes that made Sylvie feel so unpleasant. Or perhaps, she thought, he simply hadn't noticed them at all.

When there came a knock at her front door, she knew once again without having to look through the peephole who would be standing outside in the hallway. This time when she opened the door to Chase, he was still dressed in his work clothes, but as he had the last time he'd visited her at her apartment, he carried two heavily laden grocery sacks in his arms. In addition to those, he was holding a shopping bag in one hand and an oddly shaped suitcase of some kind in the other.

"I figured you'd be out of food by now," he said by way of a greeting.

Sylvie put her hand up to the doorjamb to keep him from inviting himself inside as easily as he had before. "Gee, how could I possibly be out of food when the grocery store delivered a virtual farm of stuff a week ago and claimed they had no idea who was sending it?" she asked. "Then there was that anonymous fruit basket someone sent recently, not to mention that sudden subscription to the Fish-of-the-Month Club that *I* certainly don't remember signing up for."

"How did you like the smoked salmon, by the way?" Chase asked with a smile.

She tried to ignore the way his entire face changed with that one simple expression. Honestly, Chase Buchanan was more handsome than any man had a right to be. "I gave it to Livy and Daniel," she told him. "That nutrition book you forced on me said I should avoid smoked foods."

His expression crumbled. "You're kidding. How could I have missed that?" he asked, though he seemed to be speaking to himself more than to Sylvie. "Well, no matter. I brought swordfish steaks for tonight. Completely unsmoked."

He stood in place gazing expectantly at her hand, the hand she had yet to remove from the doorjamb. But Sylvie remained firmly in place, unwilling to let him simply traipse into and out of her life whenever he pleased.

In spite of the food donations that had made her feel like a Christmas social project, Chase hadn't made any effort to contact her personally since the last time she'd seen him. And the last time she'd seen him, she reminded herself now, he'd been trying to take charge of her life. If there was one kind of man Sylvie simply could not tolerate, it was one who threatened to inhibit her freedom. And Chase Buchanan, she recalled, was a man who insisted on being in charge of everything he encountered. She would not allow herself to be swallowed up in his domination.

"Um, look," she began, trying to remain as nonchalant as she could, "I know what you're trying to do here, Chase, and it won't—"

"What is it that I'm trying to do?" he interrupted.

She blinked, confused by what seemed to be his genuine perplexity. "You're trying to insinuate yourself into my life. Mine and my baby's. And it won't work. We've been over this a million times. My life and my baby's life are none of your business."

"Oh, Sylvie, come on. I made dinner for you—once. I took you for a walk—once. I bought you a few groceries— big deal. How can you accuse me of trying to insinuate myself into your life?"

When he put it like that, it did make her sound a little paranoid, she thought. Still, she couldn't quite shake the notion that there was more to his actions of late than a sudden desire to cook healthy meals for someone. There must be dozens of other women in his life that he could be bothering. That Gwen person, for example, Sylvie recalled with a frown. Surely *she* enjoyed steamed cauliflower as much as anyone. Certainly more than Sylvie enjoyed it herself. So why was Chase picking on her?

She tried again to dissuade him. "I don't think it's a good idea for you to—"

"At least let me come in and put this stuff down," he pleaded. "My arms are getting tired."

Sylvie removed her hand from the doorjamb to run it restlessly through her hair, and Chase took advantage of her lapse to move past her and into the apartment. She opened her mouth to object, decided that any protest would be futile and closed the door behind him with a resolute *click*. By the time she turned around, he was in her kitchen unpacking the bags, and she could do nothing but stand and watch helplessly as he completed his task.

"I'll go easy on you tonight," he said as he tossed a potato into the air and caught it easily in the other hand. "No green vegetables."

She tried without success to fight back the smile that curled her lips. He just looked so wonderful standing there in her kitchen, and she couldn't deny the surge of pleasure that shot through her at seeing him again. "Thanks," she said. "I appreciate it."

Chase smiled back, thinking Sylvie looked more and more gorgeous every time he saw her. Tonight her short hair was swept back into a stubby tuft of blond, assorted mismatched pieces falling haphazardly around her face. Her bangs were mussed from the exasperated way she had handled them upon seeing him at her front door, and her nose was slightly sunburned. She wore a brightly colored tie-dyed something that appeared to have been a sack at one time but had now become a romper of sorts, tied above each shoulder and leaving her arms bare. And on her feet, he noted, she was wearing those socks again, those little cotton anklets that he found so inexplicably erotic.

"So what are you planning to subject me to instead?" she asked warily as she neared the kitchen. "Rutabagas? Parsnips? Squash?"

He shook his head. "Better than all those things put together."

"Ooo, gee, I can't imagine anything so grand," she said dryly, shivering for effect.

"One simple word says it all," Chase told her as he reached into the bag. "Eggplant."

Sylvie wrinkled her nose and mumbled something about bad karma, suggesting she must have been a persistent felon or a politician in a previous life to deserve such attention from Chase in this one.

After dinner, as their stilted, somewhat superficial conversation dragged into a series of uncomfortable silences, Sylvie began to wonder again why Chase had invaded her home. He sat at one end of the sofa, twirling a nearly empty glass of wine by the stem and staring into its golden depths with much interest, while she sat at the other end, gripping a nearly full glass of club soda so fiercely she feared she would shatter it. The quiet in the room was powerful enough to deafen her. And she couldn't for the life of her figure out what was going on between the two of them.

Feeling restless, she let her gaze wander around the room until it fixed on the shopping bag and strangely shaped leather case that Chase had brought with him to her apartment. She had forgotten them once he had set them down, but now her curiosity got the better of her.

"So what else did you bring to torture me with tonight?" she asked, trying to inject a playfulness into her tone that she was far from feeling.

His head snapped up at the sound of her voice, as if he, too, had been overcome by the uncomfortable silence in the room and was surprised to have it interrupted. "What?" he asked quickly.

She pointed at the two objects on the other side of the room. "That stuff," she told him. "Considering the vegetables you've been forcing down my throat, and the Bataan Death March you made me take two weeks ago, whatever else you brought with you tonight must be something that will drive me crazy. Otherwise, why would you bring it?"

He smiled as his gaze followed hers. "I almost forgot." He set his wine on the coffee table and went to retrieve the shopping bag and leather case, then rejoined her on the sofa, sitting a bit closer this time than he had been before. "Actually," he told her, "these are some things I brought over for the baby."

Sylvie's eyebrows shot up in surprise. "The baby? But she's not even born yet."

"This is something he can use before he's born," Chase told her. "In fact, it will contribute to his development while he's still in the womb."

She eyed him dubiously. "I thought that's what the vegetables and tofu were for."

"Those will help his physical development. These," he said, pulling a stack of compact discs from the bag, "are to aid in his spiritual and artistic development."

Her eyes narrowed even more. "Spiritual and artistic development," she repeated blandly.

He nodded, fanning the dozen plastic squares out across the coffee table with a flourish. "Jazz," he said simply. "I want you to promise me you'll play at least one of these albums for him each day. And be sure to turn the volume up loud enough for him to hear. And sit close to the speakers so that he can capture every nuance. In fact, if you have headphones, maybe you could just open them up and put them on your belly so that he could—"

"Jazz," she echoed, interrupting his grand plans.

"What else? I don't want to overpower him with anything too heavy too soon," Chase continued. "So we'll wait and do the Miles Davis and Thelonious Monk later. But this should be a good introduction for the little guy. There's some Sidney Bechet and King Oliver to get him started, and Satchmo, of course, right up through Trane and Bird, Paul Desmond, Dizzy Gillespie, Branford Marsalis...."

"Jazz," Sylvie said again.

He looked up at her as if only now remembering that she was in the room with him. "Of course, jazz. You do want him to be musically inclined, don't you?"

"Well, naturally I want her to be musically inclined. But I had something a little more..."

"More what?" he asked indignantly.

She rolled her shoulders in an uncomfortable shrug. "I don't know. I kind of saw her as a piano person."

"Fine," he said agreeably. "Next time I come I'll bring some Dave Brubeck and Earl Hines for him to listen to."

She wrinkled her nose only slightly. "Actually, I really had something more like Schumann or Debussy in mind. Jazz is just so..."

"So what?" he asked defensively.

She shrugged again, a little defensively. "So...so popular."

Chase frowned. "Oh, you mean 'common,' don't you? Well, jazz is a good sight better than that alternate garbage you listen to."

"Alternative," she corrected him. "And it's not garbage. Not all of it, anyway."

"Whatever it is, I've been listening to it on the radio lately, and I don't think much of it."

Sylvie couldn't believe her ears. Chase Buchanan, Mr. Conservative Workaholic, listening to songs by bands who condemned his very life-style? "*You've* been listening to the alternative station?" she asked.

He nodded stiffly, once.

"Why?"

"I wanted to see what kind of music you'd be exposing..." He started to say *my*, but halted himself just in time. "What kind of music you'd be exposing your baby to. And I don't think it's a good idea for a child to be hearing some of the messages those groups are promoting."

"In spite of the fact that most of those messages provide the foundation of my own beliefs," Sylvie began, "my child won't be hearing some of those groups. Not until she's a teenager. And anyway, as I've said so many times before, it's none of your business, Chase."

He was about to begin his next sentence with a phrase certain to offend her and get him ejected from her apartment right quickly— *No child of mine*—when he stopped himself a second time. That was a sure way to end this conversation immediately. He knew Sylvie didn't consider the child growing inside her to belong to anyone other than herself. And maybe, he had to concede, just maybe she was right. But dammit, he was partly responsible for the second heart beating inside her, even if the first was nowhere nearly inclined toward his way of thinking. And dammit, he intended to see to it that Sylvie's baby—his baby—had a decent start in life.

"Fine." He finally relented. "It's none of my business. But it would mean a lot to me if you'd consider giving him a well-rounded musical education. Just play one of these a day. That's all I ask. You might even find yourself learning a thing or two about music."

Sylvie opened her mouth to object, but couldn't think of a single reason she should do so. Instead, she found herself agreeing to his request before asking, "What's in the case?"

It took Chase a moment to switch gears and adjust himself to Sylvie's swift change of heart and sudden interest in the other item he'd brought with him that evening. He smiled a little sheepishly as he glanced over at the case in question. "I, uh, I hope you don't mind, but I wanted to share a bit of my own style with the little guy."

He reached for the case, clicked it open, and there, nestled in a bed of red velvet, was a gleaming saxophone. He removed it from its resting place with infinite care, its keys and curves catching the light and throwing it back in bursts of glittering gold.

"Until the other day I hadn't played this thing probably for more than ten years," he said quietly. "I don't know why I went looking for it a couple of weeks ago. I couldn't even remember where it was at first. Took me two days to find it. I'm still a little rusty, but I don't sound too bad. Apparently something like music never leaves you." He lifted an index finger to his temple. "It's all stored up here somewhere. I guess you just have to have a good reason to dig it all out."

He stroked the instrument with loving fingers, and Sylvie was reminded of the rainy, languid afternoon the two of them had spent together so many months ago. He had touched her in much the same way that he touched the saxophone, and when he wet the reed with his mouth she felt again the way his lips had simmered against her flesh when he skimmed them across her body.

"Do you mind?" he asked softly.

For one wild moment she thought—hoped—he was asking if he could make love to her that way again. Then she realized he was requesting permission to play a song, and all she could do was nod in silent assent.

But instead of lifting the instrument to his mouth, Chase met her gaze levelly with his. For a long time they only stared at each other, until he lowered the saxophone to his lap and reached across it to touch his finger to Sylvie's lips. She felt her eyelids flutter closed in response, but the rest of her body was suddenly numb, suddenly incapable of movement.

"You know, I could almost swear by the way you were looking at me just a second ago that you wanted me to..."

When his voice trailed off and he removed his hand, Sylvie opened her eyes, only to find him sitting closer to her than he had been before. "Wanted you to what?" she asked, her voice scarcely audible in the otherwise silent room.

He shook his head slowly, as if fearful of speaking his thoughts out loud. Finally he said, "You looked like you wanted me to... to make love to you again."

Instead of laughing out loud and brushing aside his suggestion as ridiculous, Sylvie felt herself blush with embarrassment. "Why would you want to make love to me?" she asked softly. "I'm a mess."

His expression changed from one of inquiry to one of incredulity. "How can you say that?" he whispered. "I've never seen a more beautiful woman than you."

She chuckled low, but there wasn't an ounce of good humor in the sound. "Yeah, right. My body is shaped like a beluga whale's about now, my ankles are swollen, my face is breaking out, I have circles under my eyes the size of radial tires because I'm sleeping so badly. My hooters have gotten so big and annoying that my bras look more like hats lately. I have veins rising up all over my body you could use to chart a course from Pittsburgh to Newark, and I—"

"And you look more beautiful now than I've ever seen you looking before," Chase repeated with a smile, curving his hand over her jaw.

The absolute certainty with which he spoke told Sylvie that he sincerely meant what he was saying. And the fact that he could feel that way about her after everything she'd said and done made her want to come apart at the seams. Suddenly none of the things about which she'd been so certain for so long seemed in any way certain at all. Suddenly she began to wonder if what she was doing—keeping Chase out of her life and the life of her child—was the right thing. Suddenly nothing seemed to make any sense at all. And suddenly she wanted nothing more than to be with him. Forever, God help her. She wanted to be with him forever.

She felt her eyes fill with tears and cursed herself for her inability to control her emotions. A single hot droplet of moisture found its way down her cheek, and immediately Chase's thumb was there wiping it away.

"What?" he asked quietly. "Sylvie, why are you crying?"

"I don't know, dammit," she responded as another tear, and then another, tumbled down her face. "Pregnant women are always emotional. It's a hormonal thing."

He placed his saxophone back in its case and pulled her into his arms. But he said nothing, simply held her while she gathered herself together.

"I don't know what's wrong with me," she said, sniffling. "All of a sudden nothing seems to be working like it's supposed to."

"And how is everything supposed to be working?"

Her words were halting and uncertain as she tried to explain. "After I got pregnant everything else was supposed to stay just like it was before. I was still supposed to go to work every day and perform my job like I always did. I was still supposed to come home every night and do the same things I'd always done, feel the same way I'd always felt."

She sniffled again, and a silk handkerchief appeared from nowhere to be pressed into her palm. "Thanks," she said softly as she wiped her nose. "That's something else that's changed, you know."

"What's that?" he asked her.

"You. You've changed."

She felt his arms tighten around her, but she wasn't sure if the gesture was a result of anxiety or affection.

"In what way?" he asked.

"After we...you know...you were supposed to go back to being just Mr. Buchanan, the guy who worked across the street and came into the restaurant for dinner, the guy who was always nice to talk to. That's it. Nothing about you was supposed to be any different. Not one single thing in my life was supposed to be different after I got pregnant."

He hesitated for only a moment before saying, "But things have changed." It was a statement, not a question, she noted, spoken with absolute certainty, as if he understood completely what she meant. As if maybe things for him had changed, too, she thought.

"*Everything* has changed," she told him. "Everything is different now. Ever since I got pregnant I haven't been able to look at anything the way I used to. I listen to music differently. I read books differently. I watch television and movies differently. I interpret conversations differently. Nothing means what it used to mean. Everything I say or do now has some extra significance because of the baby. And it's all..." She shrugged, struggling to find the right way to explain. "It's just different, that's all," she finally said. "It's not what I expected."

She sniffled again, her tears coming more readily now. Chase began to rock her softly, but said nothing more to encourage her. So Sylvie continued restlessly on her own. "And something else. I used to be absolutely fearless. Nothing frightened me, nothing. Now I seem to be scared of everything. I'm scared that the baby won't be healthy, scared that I won't be able to handle childbirth, scared that something will go wrong, scared that I won't be a good mother, scared of being alone...

"And I hate it, Chase. I hate being scared and worried all the time. But I can't seem to help it. And then there's—"

She stopped abruptly when she realized how much of herself she was revealing, when she realized she had been about to confess that her feelings for Chase were now as muddled and confused as the rest of her life seemed to be. She wanted to look up at him, but she was terrified that he'd be able to read in her face all the tumultuous emotions swirling around inside her. She wanted to ask him how he felt about her. But she feared what his answer would be.

Because a part of Sylvie—a rather large part—was worried that the reason Chase kept coming over to check up on her had nothing to do with any feelings he might have for her. He was simply concerned for her baby. His baby.

Their baby, she amended reluctantly. There was no way she could deny the reality of that any longer.

Crying came even more readily with the realization, and she palmed her eyes fretfully in an effort to stop the flow of tears. Finally she pushed herself away from him, knowing she should throw some space between them, but feeling immediately bereft without having him close by.

Chase picked up on her withdrawal immediately, and dropped his hands back into his lap. "Do you want me to leave?" he asked her softly.

Sylvie gave his question a lot of thought before replying. She wiped her eyes and blew her nose, no longer caring about how unappealing she must seem. Evidently Chase wasn't bothered by her appearance, so why should she be? Finally she looked up and met his gaze levelly with hers, wishing she understood the conflux of emotions that threatened to swallow her whole, wishing she could look into the future to discover how all this was going to turn out.

And finally she realized she had to be honest with him. "No," she said softly. "I don't want you to leave. I want you to stay. Don't leave me alone, Chase. Not tonight." She lifted a hand to touch his cheek gingerly as she added, so quietly he almost didn't hear, "Not . . . not ever again."

Ten

They were words Chase had been aching to hear Sylvie say, and now that she'd uttered them he had no idea what to think. So instead of thinking, he simply reacted. He did what he'd been wanting to do since the day she'd returned to his office to tell him she was expecting his child. He took her in his arms and kissed her. Not the drugging, passion-induced kiss of a man who has been too long without a woman's affections but a soft, sweet, searching kiss that was at once comforting and arousing. He kissed her as he would a woman with whom he shared a very intimate relationship. Because intimate was exactly how he felt about Sylvie.

"I have been wanting to do that for the longest time," he told her when he pulled away, pressing his forehead against hers. His breathing was as ragged as his heartbeat, he marveled. All because of one simple little kiss.

"You're not the only one," she replied softly.

He pulled away, surprised. "You've been wanting to kiss me, too?"

She nodded.

"But I thought you hated me. That you considered me to be nothing but a nuisance."

"Well, you *have* become something of a nuisance lately," she told him with a smile, cupping his jaw with her hand when he started to object. "But I could never..."

She couldn't even say the word, he thought, growing warm inside. Maybe there was a chance for him yet. Maybe there was a chance for both of them.

"I just...I don't know exactly what's going on with us," she said. "Like I just told you, I'm not sure about a lot of things lately, and you probably head the list. But you pop into my head a lot, especially when I least expect it. And not necessarily because of the nuisance business."

He smiled and dipped his head to kiss her briefly on the mouth again. "I'm still not quite sure what's going on with us, either," he told her. "And I can't seem to stop thinking about you. About this baby. I guess when I agreed to...to this whole bargain, I wasn't really taking into consideration everything that would come about as a result. But lately I can't seem to think of anything else."

"I know," Sylvie said. "That's how I am, too. And I wonder sometimes if I'm doing the right thing. Not just for me, but for the baby. And...and for you."

Chase tilted his head forward and cupped his hand over her nape, pulling her forehead to his again. "I know it's a lot to ask," he said quietly. "I know how you feel about all this. I know you're determined that this is your baby and no one else's. And I can respect that, I really can. But I'd like to be a part of your life while you're going through your pregnancy if you'll let me. I don't know why it's so important to me, but I...I just want to share this with you."

He heard her sigh and wondered at the sound. He couldn't tell if she was beginning to relent in her conviction that she was on her own, or reinforcing her decision to do this her way. So he decided that maybe a little more urging—of a little more personal nature—might bring her around to his way of seeing things. He kissed her again. But where before he had been responding to a softness in her he hadn't been able to resist, this time he reacted to a need of his own. This time when he kissed Sylvie, Chase meant it to last.

She melted into that kiss as if she had been the one who started it. Without warning they went from simple discussion to profound arousal. All the concern and confusion Chase had been feeling for months bubbled up with that single kiss, and before he realized what was happening he had scooped Sylvie up into his arms and was carrying her to her bedroom.

All the way there, he continued to kiss her, and all the way there, she struggled to loosen his tie. She freed it just as he was sliding her to the floor, and as soon as she found her footing she went to work on his shirt buttons. While she did that, Chase fumbled with the knots of her romper tied above each shoulder, becoming more and more frustrated when they seemed to grow tighter instead of looser with his efforts. Finally he just pushed the scraps of fabric aside, then gasped when the garment fell in a pool at her feet, leaving Sylvie completely naked save a pair of leopard-print panties.

His mouth dropped open in wonder at what he saw. He remembered a svelte, ivory-skinned Sylvie whose breasts had fit perfectly in his hands. Now she was lush and rounded and utterly, thoroughly arousing. Her breasts were much heavier and duskier than he recalled, her hips and thighs infinitely riper. Her lower abdomen, once a flat plane of delight, was now a soft mound of pink flesh that housed an extra life. Without thinking, he opened his palm over her belly. Sylvie covered his hand with hers and pressed it more tightly against her.

"Have you felt him move yet?" Chase asked.

She nodded. "Quite a few times. The activity isn't very strong yet, but I definitely know she's there."

"What does it feel like?"

"It's hard to describe. The best way I can manage is just to tell you to imagine a little creature inside your stomach poking a tiny finger into you to get your attention. It had to happen more than once before I realized what I was feeling."

Chase met her gaze levelly, still unable to fully comprehend what it must be like when she felt the baby move, then slowly swept his hand upward to curve his fingers over one breast. When Sylvie closed her eyes and sighed, he curled his other hand over her other breast, weighing both carefully before lowering his head to take one in his mouth.

She even seemed to taste different, he thought as he suckled her. But her scent—the fragrance of spices and heat and all things exotic—was still the same. He realized then that in spite of her impending state of motherhood Sylvie was still the same woman he had come to know and care for, the woman he was steadily growing to love.

The realization shocked him for a moment. Love? he repeated to himself. Sylvie? Was that possible? As he skimmed his lips up from her breast to her neck, he decided it might not be such an incredible concept after all. And then he ceased to think entirely, because she tangled her fingers in his hair and pulled his head up to kiss him, a lengthy, soul-searching kiss that left his brain patterns utterly scrambled.

As she kissed Chase, Sylvie completely undressed him, then let her fingers go wandering on their own. She explored the hard planes and grooves of his lightly muscled back and shoulders, traced the thick blue veins that wound over the backs of his hands and along his forearms. She buried her fingers in the coarse black hair scattered across his chest and flat belly, then dipped her hands lower to cup his solid hip and brush her knuckles against the long length of him.

He sucked in a rough gasp of air at her forwardness, pulling away from her kiss to gaze into her eyes. "That wasn't fair," he told her.

"Why not?" she asked.

"Because you're still dressed."

She glanced down at her panties, the only garment she still wore. "I'd hardly call this dressed."

"Nevertheless. Fair's fair."

And before she could stop him, he toppled her onto the bed and dipped his hands below the waistband of her panties, cupping her derriere firmly in his palms, bumping her pelvis softly against his.

"Oh," she murmured when she felt him so near, so ready. "Oh, Chase."

He smiled evilly, rubbing his body sinuously against hers. The action caused her to close her eyes and marvel at the unspeakably scandalous sensations shimmying through her nervous system. "Oh, my," she whispered.

"Oh, my," he echoed softly.

He seemed to be voicing his possession of something with those two little words, and all Sylvie could do was wonder what, exactly, he was stating to be his own. Then she couldn't even wonder anymore, because Chase skimmed the scrap of silky fabric from her body and pressed himself intimately into the cradle of her thighs.

"The last time we did this," he said softly, "we created life. That's a pretty awesome act to follow."

She smiled, a dreamy, almost delirious little smile, and nodded. "No telling what we'll generate this time."

"It could be dangerous."

"It could be explosive."

"It could be illegal in forty-two states."

She sighed, moving her body restlessly against his. "Oh, Mr. Buchanan, you worry far too much about details."

"I'm an architect. Details are very important in my line of work."

"Forget about your work. You need to play more."

He smiled back, the gesture making his expression become absolutely salacious. "Ms. Venner, you don't need to tell me twice."

He lowered his body to hers, burying his face between her breasts, dipping his hand to her belly and lower. She could only respond after that, could only thrash against him and murmur quiet, erotic suggestions in his ear. Suggestions he acted upon immediately and with amazing dexterity, suggestions that nearly drove her over the edge.

Just when Sylvie thought she could tolerate no more, Chase rolled their bodies so that she was seated atop him, straddling that most intimate part of him. With a wicked grin she rubbed against him, drawing a faint gasp from him that seemed to come from someplace deep within his soul. Then slowly, cautiously, she eased herself down over him.

He met her halfway with a well-angled thrust, and what Sylvie had thought was the absolute pinnacle of her sexual awakening carried her even higher.

He took her back to the place he'd taken her before, that place so unlike any she'd ever known. With one shuddering jolt after another he shattered what little composure she had left, making every raw nerve in her body explode in a white-hot demand. As he throttled inside her over and over again, he opened her up and filled her completely—filled every single empty space inside her she'd never quite been able to fill on her own. Somehow, in one final, solitary, feverish moment, Chase became a part of her. And somehow, Sylvie knew in that moment that she became a part of him, too.

And neither of them, she supposed with a final, vaguely coherent thought before sleep claimed her, would ever be the same again.

It was nearly ten o'clock when Sylvie awoke to a very annoying sound. She had been dreaming about holding her baby daughter when some kind of strange, muffled, beeping noise interrupted the tranquil vision. Gradually she opened her eyes, found herself enfolded in Chase's arms and remembered what had happened between them only a short time before. With a contented little sigh she snuggled back against his warm, naked chest and tried to ignore the sound. She hadn't awakened feeling this good for a very long time.

But the beeping that had invaded her dream continued to erupt unceasingly somewhere in the bedroom, until finally Chase, too, began to stir. He inhaled deeply, ran his hand up and down Sylvie's spine to send warm shivers through her, then opened his eyes and smiled down at her.

"Hi," he said.

"Hi," she replied.

He kissed her, a lengthy, thorough kiss, then turned his ear to the soft beeping sound that had awakened them. "What's that noise?" he asked.

She shrugged and nestled close to him again. "I have no idea."

Awareness seemed to dawn on him then, and Chase lay back against his pillow, running a restless hand through his hair. "Damn, it's my beeper," he said. "I can't believe this."

Sylvie glanced at the clock on the nightstand. "Who would be calling you at this time of night?"

He rose from the bed and began to fumble through the pile of clothing strewn across the floor in search of his pants. "I don't know," he told her. "But whatever it's about, it better be good."

When he finally located his trousers, he pulled the beeper from one of the pockets and punched a button to stop its incessant alarm, then returned to sit on the bed, where he studied the little gizmo in the light of the bedside lamp. Sylvie tugged the sheet up more securely around her and peeked over his shoulder in time to see a phone number emerge on the digital readout.

"Anyone you know?" she asked.

He sighed, an exasperated sound. "Yes. It's someone I know. And like I said, this had better be good. Mind if I use your phone?"

"Help yourself."

He hugged the receiver between his shoulder and ear as he punched the buttons that matched the number on the beeper. She was close enough to hear the phone ringing at the other end of the line, and then the muffled voice that answered it.

"Gwen?" Chase said into the receiver.

Sylvie's heart dropped to the pit of her stomach.

"What's up?" he went on.

She listened to the garbled half of the conversation coming out of her phone, but could understand nothing of what the other woman was saying.

"It's awfully late," Chase responded after a moment, his comment followed by another series of unintelligible sentences from the other side. "Isn't that something we could go over in the morning?" he asked when the barrage of static had ceased. "How about if I meet you for breakfast somewhere?"

More from the woman at the other end of the line, Sylvie noted, incomprehensible words that Chase met with a droop of his shoulders and another exasperated sigh.

"Well, if it's that important to you," he said.

Sylvie's heart dropped further.

He picked up the watch he had discarded without care on her nightstand such a short time ago, strapping it on his wrist as he nodded at something else Gwen was telling him. "All right," he said. "I can be there in about a half an hour.... Yes, that's fine.... No, don't worry about it. I'll see you in a little while.... Fine. Goodbye."

And with that he dropped the receiver back into its cradle and turned to look at Sylvie. "I'm sorry," he told her. "But I'm going to have to leave. That was—"

"A very important client," Sylvie finished for him, hoping her voice carried none of the disappointment and worry she was actually feeling.

"Yes," he said. "And there's been a problem with some of the plans I sent over for her to okay."

"A big problem?" she asked.

Chase rose and reached for his trousers again. "Actually, it's not as big a problem as she seems to think it is, but she's very concerned and wants to get all the particulars ironed out tonight. Otherwise, she says, she'll never be able to get to sleep."

Sylvie nodded. "Mmm."

He turned to face her as he fastened his pants. "What's that supposed to mean?"

She feigned confusion. "What's what supposed to mean?"

"That 'mmm' you just muttered. I'm not sure I liked the sound of it."

"Nothing. It didn't mean anything. It was just an 'mmm,' that's all."

He narrowed his eyes at her suspiciously. "Look, I can't ignore Gwen Montgomery. She's a very import—"

"I know what she is," Sylvie interrupted him. "A very important client who just so happens to be worth millions of dollars to you. And *that's* what's really very important to you, isn't it? The money, and the prestige this big schmiel project is going to bring to your company."

He looked at her as if her hair had just burst into flames. "Of course it's important."

"It's more important to you than anything else in the world, isn't it?"

"Of course it—"

He halted abruptly before finishing the statement, but Sylvie knew as well as he did what his answer would have been. *Of course it is.* Nothing mattered more to Chase Buchanan than a thriving business and tons of money in the bank. Sylvie didn't know why she had let herself forget that. She didn't know how she could have started to believe that there might be a chance for the two of them. For the three of them, she amended as she opened her palm over the part of the sheet that covered her softly rounded womb.

"It isn't like that, Sylvie," he said as he reached for his shirt and shrugged into it. "This isn't what you think."

"And what do I think it is?" she asked.

"You think I'm running out on you right now because my work is more important to me than you are. And that's just not true."

"Isn't it?"

Hastily he fastened his shirt, then wound his necktie into a perfect Windsor knot, all without ever having to look into a mirror to see what he was doing. That was Chase, Sylvie thought. All buttoned up nice and neat, without a wrinkle, without a flaw, without a care.

"No, it's not," he countered. "Gwen has a legitimate complaint about a problem I created, and it's my responsibility to take care of it."

"At ten o'clock at night? A time of day any normal human being with regular daytime office hours has the right to expect is his own?"

"It's important," Chase said again.

She fell back against her pillow in a defeated slump. "Yeah, no doubt."

"This is an isolated incident," he said emphatically as he reached for his suit jacket. "Things like this don't happen very often. Rarely in the past have my office hours extended to this late an hour."

"Yeah, before you never worked past nine," she said sarcastically. "I'm the one who served you dinner for a long time, remember? I know exactly what kind of hours you keep where your work is concerned. And you've always worked *late*.''

''That's because before I didn't have any reason not to work late. I didn't have any reason to knock off early.''

''And now you do?''

He met her gaze unflinchingly with his. ''Yes. Now I do. And I repeat: what's happening tonight is an isolated incident. It doesn't happen that often.''

Sylvie wanted to remind him that, as he himself had told her, he'd never had any Very Important Clients like Gwen Montgomery in the past. And she wanted to point out that he would probably have dozens more like her in the future as a result of his association with the powerful businesswoman. Chase's company, his career and his life were all taking off in an entirely new, infinitely more demanding direction. Sylvie knew it as well as he did. This project he was working on now would only lead to bigger and better things. And over the years, he would only become busier and busier with more projects.

If he thought he had little time now, she marveled, he wouldn't have a solitary free moment in the future. Certainly no time to devote to something as unprofitable and insignificant as a family.

''I have to go,'' he said as he bent toward her and placed a brief kiss on her forehead.

''When will I see you again?'' she asked as he pulled away.

''Tomorrow,'' he told her. ''I promise. We can meet for lunch.'' He smiled as he added, ''Maybe we could do some shopping, too. Pick up a few more compact discs for the little guy.''

She tried to smile back, but she felt none of the confidence Chase seemed to have that tomorrow would bring with it another chance for them to explore these new emotions. ''Okay, I'll hold you to it,'' she finally said halfheartedly. ''Meet me at Cosmo's at one.''

''I'll be there,'' he vowed as he kissed her quickly once more.

Then he was gone, almost as if he'd never been there, and Sylvie had never felt more alone in her life.

Eleven

Sylvie shifted restlessly from one foot to the other and watched the second hand on her wristwatch travel around the face of the clock one more time. Now it was one-nineteen, and she still had no idea where Chase was. She stood outside the entrance to Cosmo's glaring at the building across the street, wondering what had happened to him. Unfortunately, she realized, she wasn't wondering very hard. Because somehow she knew—had known since they had made arrangements the night before—that he wasn't going to be showing up for their lunch date.

Her stomach rumbled loudly, as if to remind her that she hadn't eaten since that morning. So she wandered back into the restaurant, resolved to enjoy her afternoon repast in her usual way, with a tossed salad and a bowl of soup du jour—compliments of the management—seated alone in a back booth reserved for employees on break. As she passed the bar, one of her co-workers called out her name and waved a sheet of paper at her. She took it and scanned the hastily scrawled words, her heart growing heavy to see verified in black and white what she already knew.

"Sylvie—1:15. Chase called. Can't make lunch. Will call you later."

And that was it. No apology, no excuse, no explanation, no regrets. No surprise, she thought further. With fewer than a dozen words Chase had just confirmed precisely what she had always suspected about him, despite his hot denial of the night before. His work would always come first in his life. No matter what was at stake. And he expected the world to remember that.

Sylvie sighed as she crumpled the piece of paper in her hand and discarded it in the nearest ashtray. She felt a little nudge inside her, a soft movement from the baby she had experienced so many times before.

"Yeah, I know, kiddo," she said quietly. "Daddy let us down."

The word sounded odd on her lips. *Daddy*. To her it connoted a man who came home from work at the end of a day to the squeals and laughter of children who threw themselves against him with cries of "Hooray! Daddy's home!" He was a man who hung up his suit on Friday night and didn't look at it again until Monday morning—and looked at it with dread, at that. A man who spent his evenings and weekends tossing a football with his son, or repairing a Barbie or an E-Z Bake oven for his daughters. Who argued with the Little League coach over who was out and who was safe, and with third-grade teachers about how an essay on flowers was far more important than a historical perspective of Abraham Lincoln.

Someone like her own father, she thought with a sad smile, missing the man who had passed away years ago. Someone who was nothing at all like Chase Buchanan.

"It's just as well," she told the baby moving almost imperceptibly inside her. "It's just as well we find out now exactly what kind of man Chase is. Maybe someday we'll find you a father like the one I had. Not one who only comes around when he has nothing more pressing to attend to. Not one who will lose interest as soon as the novelty wears off. The perfect father," Sylvie promised her baby. "Nothing but the best for you."

She felt another soft touch inside her and patted her belly gently. "We'll make it all right by ourselves," she whispered. "You'll see. We'll be just fine together, you and me."

She only wished reassurance for herself came as easily as it did for her unseen child.

Almost two weeks passed before Sylvie ran into Chase again. Naturally, she thought when she saw him, he would pop back into her life at a truly inopportune time. There was nothing like having the bejeebers scared out of one while one was lying on a padded table in her doctor's office being prepped for an ultrasound.

"Is this the Venner party?" Chase asked as he poked his head through the door to the semidarkened room after a single, extremely quick knock. "One of the nurses said it was all right for me to come on back."

Sylvie and the ultrasound technician—a very nice woman named Fern whose white hair held just the slightest touch of blue in the dim light—looked up simultaneously, the latter with a huge smile and the former with a forbidding frown.

"You must be Mr. Venner," Fern said, signaling Chase inside. "Come in, come in. It's so nice when the fathers can take time to be here for this. You're—"

"He's *not* Mr. Venner," Sylvie interrupted the other woman's gushing welcome.

Fern looked worried. "Oh, dear, they must have sent you to the wrong room," she told him. "You're not the baby's father?"

"Oh, I'm the baby's father," Chase said as he eased into the tiny room and closed the door behind himself. "Isn't that right, Sylvie?"

Fern turned to Sylvie for verification. "He provided the..." She paused and sighed fitfully, then decided it was pointless to try to explain that her relationship with Chase was nothing more than a biological connection. "He's the baby's father," she said with a nod of resignation. She introduced the two of them halfheartedly. "Fern, Chase Buchanan. Chase, Fern."

The other woman smiled in relief. "Well, then. You're just in time."

"Just in time to turn around and leave," Sylvie said meaningfully, propping herself up on her elbows. "How did you know I was here, anyway?"

"I saw your notation about the ultrasound on your kitchen calendar the last time I was at your place. I wanted to be here, too, and I would have mentioned it, but we didn't seem to get a chance to discuss it earlier. For some reason you haven't been answering your phone or returning calls." He eyed her with determination as he added, "And I'm not going anywhere."

"Mrs. Venner," Fern said as she held up something that looked like a plastic shower head in one hand and a bottle full of some clear, jellylike substance with the other, "we really should get started. It's imperative that I stay on schedule. Women with full bladders can be extremely touchy when they're kept waiting."

"Hey, you don't have to tell me that," Sylvie replied, her own bladder filled to near bursting at the moment. "And it's *Ms.* Venner," she added, though why she was bothering she had no idea. "I'm not married."

"Oh. I see."

Sylvie wanted to shout at Fern that she couldn't possibly see, that no sane person could even vaguely comprehend the tangle of knotted emotions and experiences that constituted her bizarre relationship with Chase. Instead, she only fell back onto the table in surrender, pushed the elastic waistband of her full, flowered peasant skirt down below her belly and pulled her baggy blue tunic up beneath her breasts, trying not to notice the way Chase studied her torso with such fascination.

"Why haven't you called me?" he asked as Fern spread the warm jelly over the lower part of Sylvie's abdomen.

She could tell he was trying to keep his voice down. She could also tell that Fern was trying to eavesdrop. So she didn't even bother to stay quiet herself.

"Because you stood me up," she said. "Remember way back two weeks ago when you were supposed to meet me for lunch? I waited for you for twenty minutes, only to be told that you called—*fifteen* minutes after you were supposed to meet me—and cancelled our lunch date. And it just reinforced something I already knew.''

"And what's that?'' he asked, his voice edged with impatience.

"That you don't have time for me. Or for my baby.''

"What?''

"It's true. Otherwise, you wouldn't have jumped out of bed at ten o'clock at night after making love to me and run off to meet with another woman.''

"Here we go,'' Fern said, her own light, carefree tone of voice obviously forced and totally ineffective in relieving the tension that was burning up the air between Sylvie and Chase.

"Another woman?'' Chase repeated incredulously. "You're nuts. Gwen's not another woman. She's a client.''

"Yeah,'' Sylvie snapped. "A very important one.''

"Now, you listen to me, Sylvie,'' Chase began again, wagging his finger at her as if she were a child. "You have absolutely no right to—''

"There's the baby's little head,'' Fern said suddenly, her quiet voice an island of tranquillity amid the stormy emotions ricocheting between Chase and Sylvie.

The couple turned to view the monitor Fern indicated on the other side of Sylvie. Immediately Chase forgot entirely what he had been about to say, because the ultrasound projection revealed a perfect outline of the baby's face in profile.

"My God,'' he whispered. "Is that him?''

"That's your baby, Mr. Buchanan,'' Fern said brightly.

"That's *my* baby,'' Sylvie countered petulantly. But she, too, was awed by the spectacle, moved beyond words at finally being able to see the little person who had been jabbing at her insides for weeks.

Chase couldn't believe his eyes. That was his child up there on that screen, he marveled. He was amazed by the detail revealed in the wavy gray lines. The head, the nose, the mouth—he could see it all. And as he was watching, the baby lifted a hand, five fingers spread open wide, and popped a thumb into its mouth.

"Looks like the little sweetheart is awake,'' Fern said.

"Is he actually sucking his thumb?" Chase asked.

The ultrasound technician nodded. "That's quite common at this point."

He ran a clumsy hand through his hair and over his face, still unable to fully comprehend the magnitude of what he was seeing. Without even realizing what he was doing, he dropped into a chair beside Sylvie and reached for her hand. Only when she squeezed his fingers hard with her own did he realize what he had done. And when his eyes met hers, he saw that she was crying.

"Pretty amazing, huh?" she said with a little sniffle.

He nodded but said nothing, not certain he could trust his own voice.

"Let's see what else we can find out about him," Fern said as she began to move the instrument around on Sylvie's belly.

Chase watched in fascinated silence as the technician honed in on two tiny feet, revealing them so clearly that he could actually count the toes. Then she pointed out a spinal column that looked more to him like a small zipper, measured the size of the baby's head and abdomen, and even revealed a perfectly shaped upper lip. She recorded the baby's heartbeat, estimated its weight and turned to beam at Sylvie and Chase.

"Everything looks terrific," she said as she gathered together a dozen still photographs that had erupted from the machine during the examination. "Did you want me to see if I can determine the baby's sex?"

"That won't be necessary," Chase said. "We already know the gender."

Fern smiled indulgently. "Oh, do you, now?"

He and Sylvie nodded in unison.

"It's a boy," he said.

"It's a girl," she chorused.

"I see," Fern replied. She handed the ultrasound pictures to Chase, who immediately began to sort through them. "Here are some shots of your son, or daughter, to show off around the office until he, or she, has a newborn photo taken at the hospital." She handed a wad of tissues to Sylvie so that she could wipe the remainder of the jelly from her torso. Instead, Sylvie used them to blow her nose. Fern's smile softened as she said, "Good luck to both of you."

As she passed by Sylvie on her way to the door, Fern paused and patted the other woman's hand sympathetically. She lowered her voice only marginally as she added, "You know, in spite of everything, something tells me that the two of you are going to be wonderful parents."

And then she was through the door, leaving Sylvie and Chase to what, for other couples, was probably a very joyous, very private moment, one to be shared in intimacy and cherished for the rest of their lives. But in light of the situation between herself and Chase, the moment seemed a bit awkward to Sylvie.

"What did she mean by 'in spite of everything'?" she asked Chase as the door clicked closed behind the technician. She wiped the last of the clear goo from her stomach and readjusted her clothing, then struggled to right herself into a sitting position. The bulk of her tummy, however, hindered her efforts.

Chase held out his hand to aid her, and she took it reluctantly, only to have him pull her up and off the table, right into his arms.

"I think," he said as he tangled his fingers in her hair, "that maybe Fern is a very wise woman. She could see right through your immature behavior—"

"*My* immature behavior?" Sylvie cried.

"And tell how much I mean to you." He brushed her cheek with the backs of his knuckles as he added quietly, "And how much you mean to me."

She emitted a single chuckle, hoping the sound was derisive, knowing it was probably closer to anxious. "You mean about as much to me as those tongue depressors over there," she said, trying to squirm free of his embrace.

But Chase only smiled and held her more tightly. "I've missed you these last two weeks," he said.

Sylvie stopped wriggling then, but made no attempt to hug him back. "Then you should have come to see me."

"I called you. I called you every day. But you never called me back."

"It doesn't take much effort to pick up a phone and dial a number. If you'd really wanted to see me, you could have stopped by the restaurant."

"I've been on site in King of Prussia for the past two weeks. I never even made it into the office. You can't begin to imagine how my work load is piling up as a result. Not to mention how much my personal life is suffering," he added meaningfully.

Sylvie tried not to look at him, tried to keep her eyes straight ahead, but that left her looking at Chase's throat. And *that* left her remembering the way he had reacted when she had kissed the little hollow at the base of his neck. So she let her gaze drop lower, and instead was reminded of just how sexy his chest was when freed of the accoutrements of civilization. Dammit, she thought. He was making it awfully hard to stay mad at him. So once again she reminded herself—and him—of precisely why she should be angry.

"So in other words," she said softly, "you've been too busy to see me."

Chase bit his lip, wishing he could contradict her, knowing that what she said was true. He had been busy for the past two weeks. Too busy to see her. But not because he hadn't wanted to. Not because he didn't care about her. It was because he had to focus all his energy right now on getting this new project for Gwen off the ground.

"It won't be like this forever, Sylvie," he said quietly. "This has all just come at a bad time. Eventually my life will be my own again."

When she finally tilted her head back to meet his gaze and saw how earnest he appeared to be, she almost backed down. Almost. "I don't think you've ever let your life be your own," she told him. "At least, not in the time I've known you. Your work always comes first. Before everything. Even before your own happiness."

"That's because my work has always been my happiness," he said. "Until now."

Sylvie wished she could believe that. She wished she could just nod her head and say she understood and then the two of them could traipse off together into the sunset. Unfortunately, she'd known too many men who said something, honestly believing what they promised was true, only to have them decide at a later date that they had made a mistake. She'd seen her sister, Livy, succumb to too many men in the same way and wind up with nothing but a heart that was bruised and battered as a result.

It wasn't that men were congenital liars, Sylvie thought. And it wasn't that they didn't truly have good intentions. It was just that they had the attention spans of children. And when they got bored with one thing, they ran off to find something more challenging elsewhere.

Chase was no different, she told herself. This prospective fatherhood business was new to him, and fascinating as a result. But as soon as he began to realize how much of his life it would demand, as soon as the charm of expectant parenthood became the reality of continual parental responsibility, he would start to back away from the baby. And away from Sylvie. She simply couldn't convince herself that he would behave otherwise.

"Just give me a chance, Sylvie," Chase told her. "Let me be a part of this with you. Let me be the one who's there for you when you need something. Let this baby be my baby, too." He kissed her temple softly and pulled away, holding her gaze with an intensity from which she couldn't break away. "Because he is my baby. The fact that I signed some stupid piece of paper relinquishing all responsibility doesn't change that."

Sylvie wasn't a hard-hearted person. Nor was she an unreasonable one. And Chase really did have the nicest green eyes she'd ever seen. She supposed there was no real reason she couldn't give him a chance. Maybe the current circumstances were a bit unusual, she decided. Maybe things would change. Maybe Chase wasn't like other men.

She sighed, feeling more confused than ever. "All right," she finally said. "I'll give you a chance. But I don't know where this is all going to lead, Chase. I can't offer you any guarantees or make any promises, and I don't want you to, either. I'm just not sure how things really are between us, and I just don't know how we're going to wind up."

He smiled, and she could see that he was relieved in spite of her confusion. "Then that doesn't make us any different from billions of other people in the world, does it?"

She wished she could feel as optimistic about what lay ahead as he seemed to feel, but something inside held her back. The Chase she had known for two years was a man who had always been defined by his career. His very life-style was dictated by the workings of his company. He was a huge success—even more so now that he was working with the indomitable Gwendolyn Montgomery—and success took constant nurturing to keep it alive. She just wasn't sure he could divorce himself from his business. And she knew his business had no place for a mate and a child.

Her thoughts were disrupted when Chase curled an arm around her shoulder and pulled her close, kissing the crown of her head before settling a hand lightly over her belly.

"How about if I buy you and the little guy the lunch I promised you two weeks ago, hmm?" he asked.

Sylvie did her best to push her worries to the darkest, dustiest corner of her brain, then nodded her assent. But one or two of her concerns refused to be penned in completely, and as she and Chase left the doctor's office and made their way to his car, she had to keep reminding herself that they were starting anew. Things would be different from here on out, she told herself.

She only hoped *different* didn't wind up meaning *demolished.*

Twelve

For the two months that followed, Chase became an active partner in Sylvie's pregnancy. He accompanied her when she went shopping for a stroller, and they selected one together. He sat with her at her kitchen table and sorted through paint chips in an effort to help her decide exactly what color would be appropriate for a gender-neutral nursery. He held her hand in the doctor's-office waiting room when she had to take her glucose tolerance test a second time, clucking sympathetically each time she emerged from another bloodletting with a new cotton ball and Band-Aid affixed to her arm. He played "A Night in Tunisia" on his saxophone for the baby's enjoyment, over and over again.

But he never once tried to make love to Sylvie.

There were the brief, chaste kisses of greeting and goodbye, and invariably she found her fingers enclosed by his whenever they walked side by side. There were countless innocent touches—his hand on her shoulder when he wanted to get her attention, a brush of his fingers on her flesh when he wiped a spot of ice cream from her lip. And she always placed his hand over her tummy whenever the baby was feeling particularly lively so that he, too, could experience something of what it was like to feel life before it was born. Those moments—those touches—more than any others, were the ones Sylvie considered the most intimate.

But the intimacy never extended beyond that.

It was something that both relieved and troubled her. When she had reluctantly agreed to give Chase a second chance, she had meant with the baby, and not with her, and she'd made that as clear to him as it was to herself. At least, that's what Sylvie had told herself at the time. But as the weeks wore on and she began to see a side of him she'd never seen before, she couldn't stop wondering if maybe she had been wrong about him after all.

Maybe he did have the makings of a family man—of the perfect father—she thought when he showed up at her apartment on the afternoon of Halloween carrying the biggest pumpkin she'd ever seen. He'd brought Three Musketeers bars to give out to the trick-or-treaters, after all.

"I hope you realize that the two of us are going to wind up eating most of these," she said of the candy as she dumped it into a huge ceramic bowl. "Five bags is way too many. I usually only get a couple dozen kids, if that many. Mostly it's just the ones who live in the building."

"Well, how was I supposed to know how many kids to expect?" Chase asked as he deposited the pumpkin onto her kitchen table and considered it with a critical eye. "I've always made sure I go out on Halloween to avoid the kids."

Sylvie gaped at him in disapproval. "Go out? How could you? You know, you're the kind of person who would have had his house egged and his trees toilet papered when I was a kid."

"Why should I be blackmailed into buying candy for a bunch of little hooligans?" he countered. "The last thing kids need is a sugar-induced rush, anyway. I'm sure the dentists of America thank me."

She shook her head at him. "You should be ashamed of yourself. The one day a year that belongs exclusively to kids, and you duck out on it."

"Well, I'm not ducking out on it this year," he reminded her. "I'm even going to carve up a great pumpkin." He tilted the gourd in question onto its side and surveyed the bottom. "How do you get these things open, anyway?"

Sylvie walked him through the finer points of jack-o'-lantern creation, patting his hand sympathetically when he gagged upon encountering the gooey stuff inside the pumpkin. He sliced valiantly, though, once she had cleaned the goop out with her own bare hands, striving for a laughingly scary face he designed using every bit of architectural knowledge he possessed. The final product was something less than what he had originally planned, however, a pumpkin with roughly three eyes, a chunky nose and very little mouth to speak of.

It was actually a very progressive jack-o'-lantern when one thought about it, Sylvie assured him as she surveyed the pumpkin on her kitchen table when Chase was finished. Very Picasso-esque. Or perhaps Warhol-esque, she decided further, tilting her head the other way. At any rate, she assured him, it was perfect for the holiday. The kids were sure to love it.

By nine-thirty the doorbell had stopped ringing, the parade of dinosaurs and Arabian princesses and hockey-masked ax murderers having slowly ground to a halt. So Sylvie and Chase microwaved two bags of popcorn to complement the mountain of leftover candy, and popped a rented copy of *The Haunting* into the VCR.

"Boy, Halloween costumes sure have changed since I was a kid," he remarked as the FBI copyright warning appeared on the TV screen. "Whatever happened to witches with construction-paper hats and ghosts in holey flowered sheets?"

"Yeah," she agreed as she tossed a piece of popcorn into the air and caught it in her mouth with a flourish. "It's a completely different holiday now. When I was a kid we ran around the neighborhood wreaking havoc until almost midnight. We'd be grounded for two weeks afterward, but it was worth it. Nowadays, kids have to go out with their parents and are usually in by nine. It doesn't seem fair."

"You must have lived in the suburbs," Chase said.

She nodded. "South Jersey. Collingswood."

"You can get away with a lot more in the 'burbs than you can living in the city," he told her. "Besides, the world was a different place then. Kids aren't safe anywhere anymore."

"Where did you grow up?" Sylvie asked him suddenly, surprised to realize how little she knew of Chase's background. Funny that the subject of their pasts had never come up before.

"North Jersey," he replied. But he said nothing more.

"Where in North Jersey?"

"Newark."

"Where in Newark?"

"A neighborhood in Newark."

"What kind of neighborhood in Newark?"

"An urban one."

"But what was it like?" she persisted.

He sighed, clearly exasperated by her questions and unwilling to answer them. He reached for the remote, turned up the sound and said, "Shh. It's starting."

Sylvie plucked the remote from his hands and clicked the movie off. "We can watch it later. It just occurred to me that we know very little about each other's backgrounds."

Chase turned to look at her, his expression impatient and clearly perturbed. "So?"

His abruptness surprised her, but she tried not to let on. "So, don't you think that's odd?"

He shook his head. "No, not particularly. I also don't think it's very important."

"Don't you want to know more about me?" she asked. "I'd like to know more about you."

Chase studied Sylvie closely, wondering why on earth she had to bring up a subject like this now and ruin what had been a perfectly good evening. The truth was, he did want to know more about her. He wanted to know every minuscule detail about her past, her present and her hopes for the future. But in order to uncover all that, he'd have to place himself at risk, have to offer up snippets of his own past in return. And the past was a place Chase simply didn't want to visit. Not now, not ever. He'd left it well and truly behind nearly two decades ago, and there was absolutely no reason of which he could conceive to dredge up lousy memories.

"You know, this is an awfully strange time for you to want to get to know more about me," he said. "I would have thought you'd want to clear all that up months ago, before you asked me to be the man who fathered your child."

He had only hoped to change the subject, to divert her attention from a topic he in no way wanted to discuss. He hadn't meant his statement to sound like an insult. But when Sylvie lowered her gaze to her lap, he realized she must have taken it as one. She picked up the remote control again, clicked on the movie and slumped back against the sofa without another word.

"Sylvie, I'm sorry," he said. "I didn't mean that the way it sounded."

"I know exactly how you meant it," she replied curtly.

"No, you don't. You misunderstood."

She didn't look at him or acknowledge his apology in any way. She only placed her thumb over the volume button to turn up the sound on the movie and whispered, "Shh. It's starting."

This time Chase was the one to snatch back the remote and switch off the film. "Don't be mad at me," he told her. "I didn't mean to hurt your feelings. I was only trying to avoid a conversation I don't want to have."

She plucked idly at a stray thread on her sweater as she asked, "Why not?"

He sighed fitfully, realized he wasn't going to get out of this as easily as he'd like, and decided to be honest. "Because my past isn't something I like to think about, that's why."

"Why not?" she asked again, still worrying the strand of thread.

Exasperated and suddenly restless, he rose and went to the kitchen to open another soda, even though his glass was still half full of the last one. He barely noticed when the carbonated beverage foamed up and spilled over the top of the glass, and he sopped up the mess absently with a paper towel as he spoke.

"Because I grew up in a pretty crummy neighborhood, that's why."

"So?" Sylvie asked, mimicking his single-syllable response of a moment ago. "My neighborhood wasn't exactly Palm Springs."

"So, it's not something I like to remember."

"Do you still have family in Newark?" she asked, her voice softening a little with the question.

He shook his head. "Not really. My mother died of cancer when I was still a kid. She worked in a chemical plant back before safety restrictions were put in place. And you know about my dad's death."

"No brothers or sisters?"

"I have an older brother I don't see too often. He's married with children—five of them—works like a dog in an auto plant, and lives about three blocks from the house where the two of us grew up."

"Doesn't sound like he hated the neighborhood all that much."

"Yeah, well, for some reason he's deliriously happy being strangled by the ties that bind. I never have been able to understand that guy."

"Maybe he saw more potential in the old neighborhood than you did."

Chase returned to the sofa and sat beside Sylvie, staring off at a place on the wall where she'd hung a photograph of herself, Olivia and Zoey, taken when they'd been on a Caribbean cruise years ago. The three of them were wearing goofy straw hats and drinking huge blue drinks with paper parasols and mountains of fruit emerging from them, and behind the three women, palm trees and a glorious blue lagoon beckoned.

"What I saw in the old neighborhood," Chase said quietly, "was block after block of crumbling old houses with no yards, kids who wore threadbare hand-me-down clothes and played with broken toys that were beyond another repair. I had to get six stitches in my knee when I was seven, because one day, when we were playing baseball, I slid into a broken bourbon bottle at the foot of the tree we used for third base in a litter-infested vacant lot. It's a lousy neighborhood," he concluded softly. "It's poor and ugly and completely lacking in opportunity. And I never want to go back to it again."

Sylvie sighed, thinking Chase's description of his childhood explained a lot about why he was so relentlessly driven in his career as an adult. Still, moving up in the world economically didn't necessarily make a person happier or more content. She wished she could think of some way to make him understand that. But something told her he'd deny any such suggestion.

"So now you live in a gorgeous condo in beautiful, tranquil Chestnut Hill, and you play with expensive toys like a red Porsche," she said.

He nodded.

"And that makes you infinitely happier than your brother could ever hope to be living with his wife and kids in the old neighborhood."

Another nod.

"Your brother is completely misguided in what constitutes happiness, is that it?"

For a third time Chase nodded in silence.

"I see."

He had opened his mouth and was about to speak—no doubt to assure her that he was, without question, the happiest man in the world, Sylvie thought—when his beeper went off. She stiffened immediately. She hated that damned noise. It hadn't sounded often in the past two months, but it had sounded. And whenever it had, Chase had always gone running off without a backward glance.

"Don't answer it," she told him impulsively, the order surprising her as much as it seemed to surprise Chase.

"I have to answer it," he told her, retrieving the beeper from the end table.

"Why?"

"Because it might be important."

"You mean like a medical emergency?"

He made a curious face at her. "No, of course not. I mean like a business emergency."

She frowned. "There's no such thing."

He contemplated the telephone number that appeared on the readout, then went to the kitchen to pick up her telephone and dial. "Sylvie, as usual, you just don't understand," he said as he waited for the party at the other end of the line to pick up.

"You're right, I don't," she told him. "I don't understand why anyone whose job doesn't revolve around medical matters or potential global catastrophe could allow himself to be on call twenty-four hours a day."

"I'm not on call twenty-four hours a day," he denied.

"What else do you call it?"

"I call it good business."

"And I call it nuts."

"Look, just because you think—" He stopped abruptly and put the phone receiver up to his mouth. "Hello, Ike? It's Chase.... That's okay, don't worry about it. I wasn't in the middle of anything important...."

Sylvie watched and listened as Chase went on to tell the other man that no, he didn't have any plans that couldn't be altered, that it wasn't too late to talk about a project the two of them were working on together and that he could meet the other man at his office in less than half an hour.

Nothing important, she thought. That's what she was to Chase Buchanan. And any plans they might ever have to simply spend time alone together were plans that he could alter without ever giving her a second thought, plans that could be changed to accommodate whatever problem might arise where his business was concerned.

She rose from the sofa silently and began to gather his things, carrying them into the kitchen to place them within his reach. As he wound up his conversation with the other man, she held his jacket open so that he could thrust his arms through the sleeves. Then she placed his loafers on the floor where he could simply slip his feet into them.

She was thinking of changing her name to something like June Cleaver or Harriet Nelson when Chase finally hung up the phone. Without a word she handed him his briefcase and a paper sack containing what was left of the Halloween candy. Then she moved to the front door and held it open for him.

Bemused, Chase only stood in the kitchen staring at her or a moment. He left the bag of candy on the counter, but efted his briefcase into his hand and approached her with much caution.

"You know, this will probably only take an hour or so," he said when he stood beside her at the front door. "I could come back, and we could still watch the movie together. It will be scarier after midnight, anyway."

"If this is only going to take about an hour, then why don't you do it tomorrow during your regular work day?" she asked.

"Because Ike is going out of town early in the morning and won't be back until next week."

"And the world economy will collapse and throw the United Nations into utter chaos if you don't get this solved tonight, is that it?"

"Sylvie..." Chase began, his voice edged with warning.

"Go," she said, sweeping her hand toward the front door. "And I'll be in bed by midnight. Don't bother to come back tonight."

He passed through the door reluctantly, then turned to face her. "I'll pick you up at six tomorrow. We can grab a bite to eat on the way and be there by seven with no problem."

She knew exactly what he was talking about, but for some reason felt compelled to give him a hard time. So she feigned confusion and asked, "Be where?"

He gaped at her. "At the hospital, of course. Surely you haven't forgotten that our childbirth classes begin tomorrow night?"

"I remember that *my* childbirth classes begin tomorrow night," she told him.

"Whatever," he said through gritted teeth, clearly striving to control his temper. Obviously he didn't have time for an argument, Sylvie thought dryly. "I'll pick you up at six."

"That won't be necessary. Zoey said she'd attend the classes with me and be my partner."

His expression hardened. "I thought we already agreed that *I* was going to be your childbirth partner," he said. She

could tell he was doing his best to keep his voice civil, bu
more than a trace of hostility still came through.

Sylvie ignored his anger, because she was too busy nur
turing her own. "No, if I recall, that's something *you* de
cided pretty much on your own, without ever consulting
me."

"Nevertheless, we had an agree—"

"But you're off the hook now," Sylvie continued relent
lessly. "Zoey can be my partner instead, and she's someone
I can count on to be there with me for all the sessions. No
to mention the actual birth."

"You can count on me to be there with you for all the
sessions," Chase told her, deflating a little. "Not to men
tion the actual birth."

She almost relented when she saw the expression of utter
betrayal on his face, almost forgot about why she was mad
in the first place. Almost. "I couldn't have counted on yo
if the sessions had started tonight and Ike had called two
hours earlier," she observed.

"But they didn't start tonight, and Ike didn't call two
hours earlier," he countered.

"That's not the point, Chase."

"Then what is?"

"The point is that I'm not the kind of woman who's
willing to sit around waiting for her man to finish up with
other things before he gets around to being with her."

"I never thought you were."

"Then why do you treat me like I am?"

"I don't."

She laughed, the sound full of disbelief and completely
lacking in humor. "You've got to be kidding. What do you
think you're doing right now? What do you think you do
every time that damned beeper goes off? You're out of here
like a shot, without ever once taking my feelings into con
sideration."

Chase opened his mouth to contradict her, but stopped
himself. Because deep down he realized she was right. He
had always left to attend to business whenever someone
called needing him. But that's because he was only called

when something was really important, when there was something he simply couldn't ignore.

"I'll be there tomorrow night," he told her.

"How can I be sure?" she asked. "And even if you are there tomorrow night, how can I be sure you'll be there next week? Or the week after that? You told me two months ago that you wanted to be here for me while I was pregnant, that you wanted to be a part of all this. But you take off without a moment's notice any time of day or night. You say you even want to be there for the baby's birth, but the minute that stupid beeper goes off, you'll leave me in midpush because one of your very important clients needs your input on some very important project."

"That won't happen," he assured her.

"How do you know?"

"I just do."

"Well, I don't."

Chase came back into the apartment then and closed the door behind him.

"You're going to be late for your appointment," Sylvie told him sarcastically.

"A few more minutes won't hurt. Something tells me you've got a lot more you'd like to say to me."

She threw him a wry smile. "And you think a few minutes will be enough?"

"Give it your best shot."

She tilted her head to offer him a considering look, then nodded. "All right. I will."

When she didn't immediately launch into the screeching tirade he had feared, Chase threw his arms open wide. "Well?" he asked. "I'm waiting."

Sylvie licked her lips once and took a deep breath. "Maybe I'm being presumptuous," she began softly, "but I had begun to think that things between us were starting to get pretty good."

"I don't think that's presumptuous," he said with a shake of his head. "Things between us *were* starting to get pretty good. As far as I'm concerned, they still are."

She nodded, but Chase didn't think she was agreeing with him.

She hesitated only a moment before continuing. "I, uh, I had even begun to think there might be some kind of future for us together. For the three of us, I mean," she clarified, splaying both hands open over her ample belly.

Chase swallowed with some difficulty. He, too, had begun to wonder if maybe there was a way the three of them could be together forever, but he'd been afraid to suggest the possibility to Sylvie just yet, afraid she would have slammed the door in his face completely and never let him set foot back into her life. Before he could say anything, however, she began to speak again.

"But now I'm not so sure about that," she said quietly. "I'm not so sure there's room for me or my baby in your life. I mean, that's what I thought before, too, back when I first asked you to be a part of all this. Hey, it's the main reason I asked you—because I knew you'd be too busy to want any part of this baby or me. Then, when we were spending more time together, I started to change my mind, started to think maybe you weren't the man I thought you were. But now I'm beginning to wonder if maybe I wasn't right all along."

"Sylvie, that's not true," he objected. "You were never right about me to begin with."

"Yeah, I think it is true," she insisted sadly. "I wish it wasn't, but it is. You were right when you said I don't understand about your work. But suddenly I think I do. I finally understand that your work is your life. Your career is like a wife, and your business is like a child you've raised from infancy. You already have a family, Chase. You don't need me or my baby to give you another one."

"You're wrong about that. I care about you—both of you—more than you could ever know."

Her brows arrowed down, and her eyes filled with tears as she said, "And I care about you, too. More than I ever thought I could care about a man. But you have to make a choice here, Chase. Something has to be more important to you—your job or..." She curved her hands open over her belly. "Or us," she concluded.

Chase didn't like what he was hearing. "Meaning what, exactly?" he asked, not sure he wanted more clarification.

Sylvie hesitated before replying, stroking the ample bulge on her abdomen as she thought. Finally she told him, "When I think about a future with you, all I can see is me and the kids sitting alone at the dinner table, waiting for you to get home while the food gets cold. I see myself making excuses for you, while you work late and I go to the recitals and baseball games alone. I hear that idiot beeper of yours going off on Christmas morning, just when junior is asking you to take him to the park to try out his new bike."

Her voice caught on the last word, and he could see that she wasn't nearly as composed as she was letting on. "Dammit, Chase," she said, the tears spilling freely from her eyes now, "whenever I try to envision you as a part of my future, all I can see is your back going through the front door."

He wanted to argue with her. He wanted to rail at her that she was so utterly wrong about her vision. That his work would never be that important to him. Never so important that he'd neglect the needs of his family.

But hadn't he neglected Sylvie's needs on a number of occasions over the past several months? Although he tried to reassure himself that he'd been there for all the important things—the visits to the doctor, the ultrasound, the bad dream—he couldn't deny that he'd missed out on more than a few opportunities to just be alone enjoying an evening with Sylvie. He'd spent the majority of his professional life completely focused on making his business the monster success that it was, and he'd done that by working sixty and seventy hours a week. It was the only way he knew how to work, the only way he knew how to live. And he couldn't jeopardize the good name of his company by neglecting it.

But he didn't want to jeopardize his future with Sylvie, either.

"Give me a chance to make this up to you," he said, reaching out to brush the tears from her face. "Just one more chance, that's all I ask."

"You asked me for a chance two months ago, and I gave it to you," she reminded him. "And I think I was more than fair. But unless you're willing to make some drastic changes in the way you work and the way you live, I can't offer up any compromises. Where family is concerned, there should be no compromises. At least if I'm on my own alone with this baby, I know my child will never be let down by a disappearing parent. But *I* won't be the one who's always trying to answer the question, 'Why isn't Daddy here with us?'"

Chase wanted to stay and hash this out with Sylvie right here and right now. But his mind was a tangle of mixed-up emotions, buzzing with thoughts he simply couldn't pin down. He'd never been so confused in his life. And he'd never felt more helpless. As much as he wanted to convince her that she was wrong, that there was no way he'd become the kind of man she described, he feared that kind of man was precisely what he had become already. He feared that was the kind of man he'd been all of his adult life. He just wasn't certain he could change.

And instead of staring straight into Sylvie's eyes and swearing she and their child would be first and foremost in his life forever, his gaze skittered to his wristwatch and he saw that he was going to be late.

"I have to go," he said quietly, something hot and searing hammering at his stomach as he voiced the words. "But I'll be here at six tomorrow to pick you up. I won't miss the class, I promise."

"Chase, I don't think it's—"

"I'll be here," he insisted. "I..."

Instead of completing whatever else he had intended to say, he reached for the door behind him and jerked it open. He was through it and had left Sylvie far behind before he allowed himself to think again. When he did, his thoughts were more than a little troubling. Because all he could do was recognize the fact that he was running away from the woman who was carrying his child. And running toward a business that was nowhere near as funny and warm and affectionate as she was, nowhere near as enjoyable to be with.

And all he could think after that was that maybe—just maybe—Sylvie was right about him, after all.

"So I guess that's it, then, huh?"

Sylvie stood outside the classroom door and looked at her

watch fretfully, moving aside to allow another happy, pregnant couple to pass by. It was after seven. Only two minutes after, but it was definitely after seven. She glanced up at Zoey and sighed.

"Well, you yourself said you couldn't count on him," Zoey told her further. "I don't see why you're so surprised now. Isn't this precisely the reason you asked me to be at your apartment tonight? Because you were afraid he wasn't going to show?"

"I was afraid," Sylvie agreed. "But I was also hoping I was wrong. I should have realized by six-thirty that he wasn't going to make it."

"And now you can be sure. Come on. The class is about to start."

Zoey took her arm and ushered her into the classroom, weaving their way through a dozen other couples—every one of which, Sylvie noted, seemed to be comprised of both a mother and a father—until they located a suitable spot in the back of the room.

"I just wish I knew what happened to him," Sylvie whispered. "I mean, he should have at least called. What if he's had an accident or something? What if traffic on the Schuylkill is at a standstill again? What if—"

"What if he's just a creep like most men are?" Zoey asked. "I'm still marveling at the fact that you got yourself knocked up by some jerk guy to begin with."

"Well, it's kind of tough to get knocked up without a guy," Sylvie noted. "Jerk or otherwise."

"Men are morons," Zoey announced. "Instead of conjuring up this fantasy of the perfect father, you should have just adopted a baby. Preferably a girl."

Sylvie waved her off. "Oh, you're such a man hater, you couldn't begin to understand."

"I'm not a man hater. I just don't trust them any farther than I can throw them."

"And with that black belt in karate you wear so proudly, something tells me you've thrown quite a few," Sylvie said with a smile.

Zoey smiled back. "Only the ones who deserved it."

The instructor entered the room then, and the class quieted. Sylvie found herself staring anxiously at the door the woman closed behind her, wondering again what had happened to Chase. She couldn't help but think that what had prevented him from attending the class tonight was significantly worse and infinitely more permanent than a life-threatening accident or an impossible-to-escape traffic snarl on the expressway.

No, knowing Chase, she forced herself to admit, if he wasn't there, it was most likely because he'd had business to attend to. Business that was no doubt very important. Obviously more important than her or her baby.

Evidently, Sylvie decided with a gut-wrenching sigh she hoped would fight back the tears that threatened, Chase had made his choice.

At 7:02 Chase was standing on the unfinished seventeenth floor of what would eventually be a high-rise office building, shivering as the cold wind buffeted him around, blowing on his fingers in an effort to thaw them and holding fast to a hard hat that was two sizes too small. He was trying to listen to Ike Guthrie describe what the other man thought an insurmountable problem, and cursing himself for leaving his cellular phone in the car.

He had been standing like this for nearly two hours, and was ready to jump over the side of the building if that was what it took to put an end to Ike's ceaseless chatter. He wanted to be with Sylvie, wanted to know what was going on in their childbirth class that he was missing. He hoped she would take notes and go over them with him later. However, he knew there was little chance of that. Sylvie was probably sitting with her friend, Zoey, and the two of them were probably whispering about what a lousy creep he was, in no way a suitable man to be anyone's father.

"Ike, I really have to get going," Chase said suddenly, interrupting whatever it was the other man was saying.

Ike Guthrie was a big, blond bear of a man, someone totally focused on the enterprise at hand, someone Chase thought he'd probably be better off not offending. The project on which the two of them were working together was an important one, one that had commanded a good bit of Chase's time and attention since he'd agreed three months ago to complete it. What he hadn't realized then, however, was just how overwhelming the task was going to be when added to his other commitments. What he hadn't realized was that it was going to cut into so much of his time with Sylvie.

"Go?" Ike cried, clearly appalled by the idea. "No way. You're not going anywhere. Not until we get this figured out." He, too, lifted his bare hands to his mouth to blow some life back into them. "Look, I don't like being up here any more than you do. And I canceled my trip to D.C. because of this. Now you say you have to leave? To go where? What could be more important than this?"

"Would you believe a childbirth class?" Chase asked.

Ike shook his head. "No, I wouldn't. Give me a better reason."

Chase wanted to shout that there was no better reason, that learning how to bring a baby into the world was about as major as reasons got. But Ike had postponed a crucial business trip today after a snag neither of them had anticipated had threatened this project. How was Chase supposed to explain that he needed to get away for something like a childbirth class, something that was so utterly outside the other man's realm of experience?

When Chase said nothing more to counter Ike's comment, the other man pointed a finger at the blueprints on the table before them and began to talk again. Chase scarcely heard what he was telling him as he went on and on about the significance of some structural flaw. All he knew was that it was dark, he was cold, and somewhere out there in the city there was a woman who was nurturing a child in her womb, a woman who was learning how to bring that child into the world and to care for it once it was here. A child that was his, too.

And here he stood, miles away, unable—or unwilling—to take part in that miracle. Sylvie was right, he thought. She'd been right all along. He'd be a lousy father and an even worse husband. His job was too demanding, his company too successful, for him to give either anything less than all he had to give. And Sylvie and her baby were too important for him to give either of them less than his all. If he split himself in half, he'd wind up neglecting both career and family, and probably lose everything in the bargain.

Being a businessman was what he excelled at. It was what he'd been for nearly half his life. This fatherhood stuff was iffy under the best of circumstances. There were no guarantees that he would ever be any good at it. Hell, he thought, if the past couple of days were any indication, he'd already failed miserably. He couldn't be counted on to perform even the most basic function like attending a childbirth class. He'd promised Sylvie he'd be at that class—he'd given her his word. And if he couldn't keep his word to her, then where did that leave his son later in life? What happened on those occasions when the boy was there to witness his father's neglect? He was bound to wind up hating Chase's guts.

Sylvie and her child deserved better, Chase thought. Hell, they deserved the best. They deserved a man who would be there for them at the drop of a hat, a man who could be counted on to keep his word. And that man obviously was not Chase Buchanan. Otherwise he'd be with her now, performing the simple task of helping her learn to breathe and bring their child into the world.

"Chase, are you listening?"

Ike's voice was hard and irritated, and Chase could tell he was quickly losing patience.

"Yeah, I'm listening," he said. *Not to you,* he thought further, *but I'm listening to the most important message being delivered here.*

That message was that he was nothing at all what a good father should be, and he'd be better off remembering that. He should stick to what he knew, he told himself, and quit trying to be what he was not.

And what he was not, he realized then, was the perfect father that Sylvie Venner and her baby should have.

"Listen, Chase, are you in on this project or not?" Ike demanded. "Make a choice and stick with it."

Chase hesitated for a moment before responding, but finally replied sadly, "I'm in. On this project, anyway."

Thirteen

Sylvie was out Christmas shopping with Zoey and Olivia on a rare weekday with the three of them off from work when she first noticed the odd little pain in her lower abdomen. Since her due date of December fifteenth was still three weeks away, however, she ignored the sensation, dropping an idle hand to her belly to gently rub it away. But the sensation wouldn't go away. Neither did it grow stronger, though, so she didn't bother to mention it to her companions. No doubt she was just experiencing some kind of weird preliminary thing, she told herself, some kind of dress rehearsal her body was putting on to prepare itself for the real labor that would follow in a few weeks.

However, an hour later, when she picked up a spun-glass ornament in one of the mall's department stores only to watch the delicate star shatter in a million pieces on the floor because a much sharper pain racked her midsection, she began to understand that her body was demanding her appearance at something more than a dress rehearsal. What this was, she realized with no small amount of panic, was an opening night premiere. A premiere for which she was in no way prepared.

"Oh, boy," she said when a second pain shot through her several moments later.

"What's the matter?" Zoey asked as she joined her friend near the elaborate Christmas-tree display. She frowned when she noticed the broken ornament on the floor. "Oh, Sylvie, honestly," she said, stooping to gingerly pick up what she could of the mess. "You're such a klutz sometimes."

"Oh, boy," Sylvie repeated on a small gasp under her breath.

"What's wrong?" Olivia asked as she joined them.

"Oh, Sylvie's just being a butterfingers again," Zoey said.

"Actually, I, uh," Sylvie began, "I'm not entirely sure, mind you, having never experienced such a thing before, but . . . I think I might be going into labor."

"That's silly," Zoey told her. "You're not due for another three weeks. You won't go into labor until next week at the earliest, and even that would be very unusual. Statistically speaking, the vast majority of women—"

"Oh," Sylvie said again, gripping her belly with her other hand.

Olivia narrowed her eyes in concern. "Walk around a bit," she suggested. "Maybe that will help alleviate whatever it is you're feeling. Let's walk down to the café and have something to eat."

Sylvie nodded. "Okay. But what about the broken ornament?"

"Just leave it," Olivia told her. "This kind of thing must happen all the time. They'll clean it up and write it off."

"But I should pay for it. I broke—"

"*Leave it,*" Olivia repeated in the voice of a militant dictator.

And that was when Sylvie began to get very concerned. Because her sister never used that tone of voice unless she was worried about something.

"I am going into labor, aren't I?" she asked her companions. They were nurses, after all, she reminded herself.

Nurses in a maternity ward. They must recognize a woman in labor when they saw one.

"Maybe," Olivia said, hooking her sister's arm through her own. "But maybe not. It's probably false labor. Walk with me. See if that helps."

The two women began to walk toward the escalators with Zoey bringing up the rear.

"How bad is the pain?" Zoey asked.

"Not too bad," Sylvie said. "About as bad as menstrual cramps. What's wrong? Why do you guys seem so worried?"

"Are you having any other discomfort?" Olivia asked her. "Is this the first time you've felt anything like this?"

"Well, I woke up with a backache this morning, and it's pretty much stayed with me. And I had a few cramps after breakfast. Why?"

"Are the cramps you've been feeling regular?"

Sylvie shook her head. "No, they come and go. Why?" she demanded again. "Why do you sound so worried?"

"You just shouldn't be going into labor yet, that's all," Olivia told her. "You're only thirty-seven weeks."

"But that's only three weeks early," Sylvie objected. "That's not too bad, is it? They say any time between two weeks before your due date and two weeks after is normal. So really, I'm only a week early."

"I'm sure everything is fine," Olivia told her. "But let's see if we can't just hold this off a little while longer."

They bypassed the café when Sylvie said she didn't think she could sit still, and headed outside into the cold November afternoon. The bracing fresh air and a jaunt around the parking lot a couple of times ought to do it, Olivia decided. Then they could grab a bite to eat and go to the movie they'd been planning to see that afternoon.

But Sylvie's baby evidently had other ideas about that. Because three hours after the episode with the Christmas ornament, her pains were growing more severe, and they were coming in a more regular pattern.

"I don't know about this," Zoey said as Olivia helped Sylvie down to the sofa in her sister's living room. "I think what we have here is true labor."

Olivia nodded, her expression clearly concerned. "I think you're right. How do you feel, Sylvie? Do you want to lie down for a little while? Think you could eat something light? You're going to need all the energy you possess for this."

"I don't want to lie down," she said, gripping her abdomen when another cramp shot through her midsection. "Whoa, that was a new one."

"I'm calling your doctor," Olivia said as she went to the kitchen and scanned the list of emergency phone numbers attached to Sylvie's refrigerator. "She may want us to come on into the hospital now."

Sylvie nodded, too anxious to argue. God, it was going to happen, she thought. It was really going to happen. She was finally going to meet the little person who'd been living inside her, beating the hell out of her organs for nearly nine months. She was about to lose her solo status and become a two-person act. The realization should have comforted her, she told herself. But all she could think about was Chase, and the fact that what was going to be a duo should be a trio instead.

He hadn't once tried to get in touch with her after leaving her apartment on Halloween. In spite of the things she'd said to him that night about his workaholic way of life and her fear that she and the baby would never fit into it, she had been surprised that he had made the decision she'd demanded. Surprised, too, that he had decided in favor of his career. Why that should surprise her, she didn't know. Hadn't she told herself all along what kind of man he was? Hadn't she been convinced from the start that he would want no part of a wife or child?

But something inside her still suspected there was more to Chase Buchanan than he let the outside world know. During the time they'd spent together she'd seen something in him she never would have suspected. She'd seen a soft side, a caring side, a side that seemed to thrive and blossom in the presence of simple human companionship. Something told her that his career didn't necessarily have to come first in his life. It was just that overworking himself was the only way he knew how to live.

Maybe no one had ever shown Chase there were other ways to be happy, Sylvie thought. Maybe he'd never come to realize that one could take pride in more than what one had created professionally. Maybe he just needed a good teacher to show him the way, that's all. She wondered why she hadn't understood that before. Maybe she'd been wrong in denying him another chance. Maybe one more chance was precisely what he needed—and deserved—now.

"Call Chase," Sylvie told Zoey when another, stronger pain made her gasp. "His business card is in my wallet. I'm sure he's still at his office this time of day. Call him and tell him he's about to become a father."

"Do you think he'll come?" Zoey asked as she reached for her friend's purse. "He didn't show up for the classes. What makes you think he'll be there for the main event?"

"I'm giving him one more chance," Sylvie said. "If he blows this one, then it's definitely over."

"If you ask me—" Zoey began.

"I'm not asking you," Sylvie interrupted. "I'm telling you. Phone Chase. Now. Tell him ... tell him that his future is calling."

Chase was in his conference room, utterly absorbed in a *very* important meeting with not one but two *very* important clients when he heard a vaguely familiar noise, something he hadn't heard for quite some time.

Plink-plink-plink-plink-plink.

His heart raced wildly as he glanced up at the conference-room windows, expecting to see Sylvie standing on the other side beckoning to him as she had done more than eight months ago. Instead he saw a very tall red-haired woman tapping on the glass. Tapping with long, red-lacquered fingernails that seemed capable of scratching a man's eyes out—and an expression that suggested she meant to do just that. Behind her, his secretary, Lucille, was shaking a reproving finger at the stranger and seemed to be shouting.

In much the same way Sylvie had done before, the woman crooked a finger at him meaningfully, totally disregarding both Lucille and the other people in the conference room. Chase shook his head, indicating he had no intention of being intimidated by some stranger, and went back to making a deal that would put his company at the front of the architectural design race. He might even get national coverage for this one, he thought as he bent his head back down to the plans.

Before he realized what was happening, the redhead was through the conference-room door with Lucille right on her heels and still shouting at her, and Chase felt strong fingers grip his shoulder and jerk him back hard. When he turned, he was staring into an arresting pair of green eyes that dared him to challenge their owner, and any objection he was about to utter was completely lost.

"Who the hell are you?" he demanded instead.

"Hey, Buchanan," the woman said. "You're coming with me. You've got a little date with your destiny."

Lucille darted out from behind the woman and said, "I've called security, Chase. They should be here any minute."

"And could you puh-*leeze* call off this guard dog?" the strange woman asked, shouldering Lucille back out of the way. "Honestly, she's been telling me for hours that you're not taking any calls, then when I come to see for myself, she tries to wrestle me to the ground until the cops get here. She's not very polite."

"Lucille, it's all right," Chase said.

"Grab your coat," the redhead instructed further, "and we can be gone by the time the Mickey Mouse Patrol gets here."

"Who *are* you?" Chase asked again.

"Name's Zoey, but you can think of me as the archangel Gabriel. I'm here to tell you you're about to become a father. Now where's your coat?"

Chase gaped at her and replied automatically, "In my office. Through there."

He pointed at his office door without even realizing what he was doing, then watched dumbfounded as Zoey passed through the door and emerged with a bundle of clothing.

"Sylvie's having the baby?" he asked her.

"Yup."

"But... but it's too early. She's not due for three more weeks."

"Surprise!" Zoey said sardonically as she threw his jacket and overcoat at him. Chase caught them just before they would have hit him in the face. "Lesson number one about babies," she continued, "and you're going to have a lot more of these lessons to learn in the years to come—never expect one to do what you think it's supposed to do."

"But—"

"Sorry, ladies and gents," Zoey said to the other people present in the conference room, "but Mr. Buchanan will be leaving the building now and won't be available until next week. He's having a baby."

And the next thing he knew, Chase was struggling into his jacket and coat, and running after a redhead who called herself Gabriel.

They arrived at the hospital when Sylvie's labor pains were coming fewer than five minutes apart. Chase couldn't remember anything of the drive to the hospital, couldn't even recall if it had been him or Zoey who had done the driving. He'd been too wrapped up in what was happening, too stunned by the knowledge that he was about to become a father.

A *father*. The word was strange to him still.

It implied a man so much different than he was himself. Someone who was relaxed and easygoing, to whom understanding children was an innate trait. He thought about men he'd seen occasionally with toddlers strapped to their backs in backpacks, or pushing brightly colored strollers through the park. He wondered what it would feel like to hold a tiny little hand in his own and know that he was responsible for the child at the other end. He honestly couldn't imagine himself doing any of those things.

But he found himself profoundly wanting to give them a try.

He thought, too, about his own father, a man who had worked two jobs to make ends meet, who hadn't been there for his sons nearly as often as Chase and his brother would have liked. Hell, he'd hardly known his own father, the old man had been gone so much. Was that how Chase wanted his own child to feel about him?

He didn't think Sylvie looked so good when he came bursting into her LDR room. Her hair was damp with sweat, her face was pale and she had an oxygen mask over her mouth and nose. Her eyes were closed and smudged with faint purple crescents below, and she seemed to be sleeping. Another woman with dark hair stood on the other side of the bed holding Sylvie's hand, but he only acknowledged her with a brief nod before dropping his hand to Sylvie's cheek.

Immediately she opened her eyes, and through the clear plastic he could see her smile. "You made it," she said, her voice sounding weak and hollow through the mask. "I knew you would."

"I had no choice," he told her. "That was some storm trooper you sent to retrieve me."

Sylvie shook her head slowly. "You didn't come because Zoey's such a bully. You came because you wanted to be here."

"Yes," he said, stroking his hand over her forehead to brush her wet hair back from her face. "I want to be here for you. And for the baby. And for me. What can I do?"

"Hold my hand," she said.

He took her hand in his at once, and felt her squeeze gently.

"Chase, this is my sister, Olivia," she whispered, clearly growing fatigued already. "Livy, this is Chase, the father of my baby. You two be nice to each other, you hear?" Then her eyes flickered closed again.

"How's she doing?" he asked the woman on the other side of the bed.

Olivia shrugged, apparently resigned to Chase's presence. "Better than a couple of hours ago. She was hoping for a natural birth, but the pain was too much for her to tolerate. She asked for an epidural about a half hour ago. It shouldn't be much longer now."

"She's not in any pain, is she?" he asked. He didn't know if he could handle seeing Sylvie suffer.

"Not anymore." Olivia released her sister's hand and came around the foot of the bed to squeeze Chase's shoulder gently. "She'll be fine now that you're here. I'm going to go get a cup of coffee. It's been a long day.'' She turned when she reached the LDR-room door and added, ''I'll make sure Zoey and Daniel leave you two alone.''

Daniel must have been the other big lug out in the waiting room, Chase thought as he pulled up a chair and sat beside Sylvie's bed. The one who looked as if he wanted to beat the hell out of him for something. He admired the magnitude of love and protectiveness these people seemed to feel for Sylvie. Then he recalled his own feelings for the woman who clung to his hand, even in sleep, and wondered how he could have questioned any other reaction to her.

It was several hours later that she finally gave birth to their daughter. A girl, Chase marveled, watching with astonishment as the messy bundle of baby emerged from inside Sylvie. He rubbed a hand over his face as the doctor wiped the infant off, not quite able to believe the sight he had witnessed, then felt something warm trickle down both cheeks. He wiped away the strange sensation and palmed at his eyes.

Never, he thought, not if he worked relentlessly for the rest of his life, would he ever be able to contribute to the creation of something as magnificent as that again. No office building, no fashion mall, no high-rise condos could ever come close to the perfection of the tiny baby the doctor placed in Sylvie's arms.

And suddenly, none of what he had spent his adult life doing seemed in any way important. Not one bit of it.

This was what it was all about, he thought as he took his place at Sylvie's side, hugging her close as he curled his big index finger under all five of his daughter's. This was the secret to life. Nothing else mattered. Just Sylvie and the baby and the way the two of them made him feel. It was as if Chase had an epiphany right there on the spot. As if the skies opened up and someone handed him the most beautiful gift he could ever imagine. It was all right here, he thought. In this tiny room, he had everything he could ever want, everything he would ever need. Everything else faded to nothing.

"She's beautiful, isn't she?" Sylvie asked with a sob, not even trying to halt the flow of tears that tumbled freely down her cheeks.

The baby in her arms was wriggling and mottled and just slightly tinged with blue. Her mouth was wide open as she cried out at the ignoble disservice just done to her in yanking her out into the real world. Her head was rather conical in shape, and she was still stained with the remnants of the womb. And Chase knew without question that he'd never see a more beautiful sight.

"She's gorgeous," he agreed, the two words about all he was able to manage.

"Genevieve Ruth," she said softly. "Ruth was my mother's name. What do you think?"

Chase nodded. "Genevieve Ruth Buchanan. Sounds great."

Sylvie looked up at him, her expression anxious. "You think she should have your last name?"

"I think she should have *our* last name," Chase said. "That is, if you want to take my name after we get married. But if you want to stay Sylvie Venner, I certainly understand."

She opened her mouth to speak, closed it again, then opened it once more. But when no words emerged, Chase smiled.

"Okay, if you want to stay Sylvie Venner after the wedding, then our daughter can be Genevieve Ruth Venner-Buchanan. Makes her sound like an heiress."

Sylvie smiled. "Yeah, it does." Then her smile faltered. "But what exactly will she be inheriting?" she asked softly, smoothing her finger over Genevieve's cheek to soothe the baby's crying. "From her father, I mean."

Immediately the baby ceased her wailing and turned her head toward her mother's hand. Sylvie and Chase laughed together.

"I'm serious, Chase," Sylvie said when she turned to look at him again. "She deserves a father who's going to be there for her every step of the way. And I deserve a husband who won't compromise my love for him with some stupid little miracle of the electronic age. I won't have you *and* that beeper living under my roof."

"From now on, the beeper stays in the glove compartment from five in the evening to seven in the morning," he vowed. "Ten hours a day to business, Monday through Friday. No more, no less. That's what I can promise you."

"How?" she demanded. "How can you promise me something like that when you've done nothing but go back on your word before?"

"I know," he told her. "And I'm truly sorry that I had my priorities so screwed up before. But I can do this now. I can do it by completing two mergers."

"*Two* mergers?"

He nodded. "One with you, and one with Ike Guthrie."

"Who's Ike Guthrie?"

"He's an architect from Pittsburgh who's looking to expand. A few weeks ago he suggested the two of us combine our energies and merge our companies. At the time I thought it was a lousy idea. I didn't want to surrender that much of my business to someone else.

"But now," he added, smoothing his hand over the soft down covering Genevieve's scalp, "now I think it's a fabulous idea. Ike and I seem to work well together, and he's even more ambitious than I am. He's perfectly willing to take the brunt of the pressure. It would cut my professional obligations in half and give me a lot more time to spend with my wife and children."

He looked at Sylvie then, his eyes full of something she was afraid to hope was real. "Because I'm very much hoping that you'll agree to be my wife," he told her softly. "And if we can, I'd like to have more children with you. If that's okay with you, of course."

"Why?" she asked, scarcely able to believe what he was saying to her. "Why would you want to do that?"

He shook his head in amazement that she didn't already know the answer to that. "Because I love you," he said simply. "I think I've loved you since the day I walked into Cosmo's and saw you working behind the bar. And I know I'll love you until the day I die. I can't live without you. Or our baby. I want us to be a family. I want to spend the rest of my life loving both of you. And anybody else who might come along. Think you can find it in your heart to give me one last chance?''

"Oh, Chase," Sylvie cried, her tears erupting again. She cupped his jaw with trembling fingers. "I love you, too. And you don't need any more chances. You've passed the test with flying colors already. I knew you'd be the perfect father for my baby. I just knew it."

She pulled him down for a soul-shattering kiss, then sighed with utter contentment as she pressed her forehead to his. "I just never thought I'd be lucky enough to find the perfect husband, too."

Epilogue

Sylvie emerged from her bedroom on Christmas morning wearing white, only to find the most wonderful gift in the world waiting for her under her tree. Chase stood resplendent in one of his dark power suits, a sprig of holly and berries tucked into the buttonhole of his lapel. Beside him was his brother, Alex, whom she had met for the first time the week before, and in his arms was their daughter, Gennie, wearing a tiny red velvet dress and minuscule black patent Mary Janes. Olivia, also wearing red velvet, completed the picture, along with the justice of the peace Chase had pressed into commission. Elsewhere in the room were assorted friends and relatives, some new to Sylvie, some old, but every last one smiling.

It was a wedding unlike any she had ever dreamed of having. Simply because she had never dreamed she could be this much in love. Nor had she ever dreamed that any man, especially one as perfect as Chase, existed who would love her so in return.

And after Sylvie and Chase had exchanged their vows and encouraged their guests to begin the festivities, they gathered up their daughter and slipped out unnoticed to spend the rest of the holiday in splendid seclusion. They'd had so little of that together over the past few weeks, with visitors and well-wishers coming and going all the time. And somehow, neither of them thought a lifetime would be nearly enough for everything they wanted to do.

However, they decided as they tucked a sleepy Genevieve into bed much later that night, a lifetime seemed like a very good start.

*   *   *   *   *

DREAM WEDDING
by Pamela Macaluso

Don't miss JUST MARRIED, a fun-filled series by Pamela Macaluso about three men with wealth, power and looks to die for. These bad boys had everything—except the love of a good woman.

* * *

"What a nerd!" Those taunting words played over and over in Alex Dalton's mind. Now that he was a rich, successful businessman—with looks to boot—he was going to make Genie Hill regret being so cruel to him in high school. All he had to do was seduce her…and then dump her. But could he do it without falling head over heels for her—again?

Find out in DREAM WEDDING, book two of the JUST MARRIED series, coming to you in May…only in

Five unforgettable couples say "I Do"... with a little help from their friends

Always a Bridesmaid!

Always a bridesmaid, never a bride...that's me, Katie Jones—a woman with more taffeta bridesmaid dresses than dates! I'm just one of the continuing characters you'll get to know in ALWAYS A BRIDESMAID!—Silhouette's new across-the-lines series about the lives, loves...and weddings—of five couples here in Clover, South Carolina. Share in all our celebrations! (With so many events to attend, I'm sure to get my own groom!)

In June, **Desire** hosts
THE ENGAGEMENT PARTY by Barbara Boswell

In July, **Romance** holds
THE BRIDAL SHOWER by Elizabeth August

In August, **Intimate Moments** gives
THE BACHELOR PARTY by Paula Detmer Riggs

In September, **Shadows** showcases
THE ABANDONED BRIDE by Jane Toombs

In October, **Special Edition** introduces
FINALLY A BRIDE by Sherryl Woods

Don't miss a single one—wherever
Silhouette books are sold.

Silhouette®
™

AAB-G

INTIMATE MOMENTS® Silhouette™ Extra

CODE NAME: DANGER

Because love is a risky business...

Merline Lovelace's "Code Name: Danger" miniseries gets an explosive start in May 1995 with

NIGHT OF THE JAGUAR, IM #637

Omega agent Jake MacKenzie had flirted with danger his entire career. But when unbelievably sexy Sarah Chandler became enmeshed in his latest mission, Jake knew that his days of courting trouble had taken a provocative twist....

Your mission: To read more about the Omega agency.

Your next target: THE COWBOY AND THE COSSACK, August 1995

Your only choice for nonstop excitement—

INTIMATE MOMENTS® Silhouette™

COMING NEXT MONTH FROM

SILHOUETTE®

Desire®

The next installment of the delightful

HAZARDS INC. series

THE MADDENING MODEL
by
SUZANNE SIMMS

Sunday Harrington was beautiful, brainy...and Simon
Hazard found her unbearable—until the pair got stranded in
the jungle and he learned that there was more to her than
met the eye.

HAZARDS, INC.: Danger is their business; love is
their reward!

And now for something completely different...

SPELLBOUND
ROMANCE

**In April, look for
ERRANT ANGEL (D #924)
by Justine Davis**

Man In Crisis: Dalton MacKay knew all about grief. It consumed him...until a troubled teen and a well-intentioned teacher barged into Dalton's very private life.

Wayward Angel: Evangeline Law was no ordinary woman—or educator. She was a messenger of hope in a seemingly hopeless case. And her penchant for getting too involved reached the boiling point with sexy Dalton....

**Get touched by an angel
In Justine Davis's ERRANT ANGEL,
available this April,
only from**

SILHOUETTE... Where Passion Lives

Don't miss these Silhouette favorites by some of our most distinguished authors! And now, you can receive a discount by ordering two or more titles!